喚醒你的英文語感！

Get a Feel for English !

喚醒你的英文語感！

Get a Feel for English !

Telephoning

搞定商務電話

總編審⊙王復國
作　者⊙Bill Hodgson

Biz Telephoning

寫得眉飛色舞，英文電話一來就瞬間破功？本書涵
所需的電話英文全範疇，強化國際商務對話智商，
成溝通實力！

330 個實用電話句型
30 場擬真對話
18 組免緊張聽力小試
2 組超好用電訪計劃表

貝塔語言出版
Beta Multimedia Publishing

附2片實戰CD

企業菁英推薦

隨著今日全球經濟結構的變化、網路科技的推波助瀾，全球企業國際化的腳步正如火如荼地展開，國際業務之利基和焦點，就在如何利用商務電話「開發潛在客戶」和「迅速且及時地」回應客戶。

對國際商務專業人士而言，國際顧客關係管理中最重要的一環就是「商務電話」的臨場實戰經驗累積，一般商務運作可從 Email 往來中達到問候與釐清業務項目之功用，但與國際買家雙方最後權益之協商，其工具和方法則肯定需經過數次商務電話談判才能達到敲定合作關係與訂單之目的。

個人從事服務業、海外業務開發及擔任國際專業經理人總計近二十年之歷練，深刻體驗到一個業務贏家之思維，平日需具備扎實的專業技術和購置有效益之工具書並積極培養商業上之獨到眼光，貝塔出版之《搞定商務電話》一書，絕對是一本從事國際商務的專業人士首選必備工具書。

本書編輯群以細心且循序漸進的方式編排商務電話所需之說、寫、讀、聽英語句型與會話；其中，「文化小叮嚀」單元將各地文化習俗和禮節列為讀者應注意之要點，具備世界觀之考量，更增添本書實用效益。

盟訊實業業務經理

PREFACE

Have you ever heard or seen an English word or phrase, and then thought to yourself, "I know that word! I've seen it before, but ... I just can't remember it!" If you have, it probably means that you don't really "know" that word yet, you've just "encountered" it. It may have been in your short-term memory for a while, but now it's gone.

Most of us, when we encounter a new word or phrase, look the phrase up in a dictionary, and then repeat it to ourselves several times in an attempt to memorize it. This approach is largely ineffective. Language experts say that we need to be exposed to a new word or phrase at least five times—in different contexts—before we will be able to remember it, and before it will go into our long-term memory.

The late Dr. Pimsleur, one of the world's leading experts in applied linguistics, developed a theory to explain this phenomenon, which he called "Graduated Interval Recall." This theory says that target words and phrases need to be introduced at periodic intervals for them to move from short-term into long-term memory. Dr. Pimsleur also advocated mastering the "Core Vocabulary" of any language—those words and phrases that occur most frequently, and which from the foundation of language proficiency.

Beta's Biz English series was designed with Pimsleur's theories about language and memory in mind. In this book on biz telephoning, readers are taught the 330 core phrases for business telephoning. Each phrase is introduced once, along with a sample sentence. Then, many of the phrases are repeated again in the "Show Time" dialogue in each chapter, where readers can see how the phrase is used in larger context.

It's often said that "repetition is the mother of mastery," and there is no area where this is more true than in learning a foreign language. Devote yourself to studying the content in this book, and to listening to the accompanying CDs, and you won't just have encountered the material, you'll have really learned it!

Happy Studying,

Mark Hammons

英文主編序

你有沒有曾經聽到或看到某個英文單字或用語，然後心裡想：「我認識這個單字！我看過，可是……我就是想不起來！」如果你有這種經驗，就表示你還沒眞正「認識」這個字，你只是曾經「遇見」它。也許這個字存在你的短期記憶裡有那麼一下子，不過現在卻煙消雲散了。

遇到新的單字或用語時，我們大部分的人會查字典，然後複誦個幾遍試圖背起來，但這種方法的效果十分有限。語言專家指出，我們要在不同語境中接觸到一個字或詞至少五次才能把它們記起來，我們的長期記憶也才能加以儲存。

已故的保羅．皮姆斯勒博士是全球應用語言學界的翹楚，他發展出一種理論來解釋此現象，他稱之爲「漸進式間歇回想」。這種理論認爲目標單字或用語必須經過週期性間隔導入，才能從短期記憶化爲長期記憶。皮姆斯勒博士也提倡熟悉任一語言裡的「核心字庫」，也就是最常被使用、構成精通該語言基礎的字詞。

貝塔的商用英文書系是依皮姆斯勒博士針對語言和記憶的理論設計而成。在這本以商務電話爲主題的書籍裡，讀者會學到 330 個使用電話所需的核心句型。每種句型會附一個例句呈現，而其中許多句型會在每章「Show Time」對話單元中重複出現，這時候讀者能夠領略如何把這類句型用在更廣的語境中。

常有人說「反覆能造就精通」，這句話用在學習外語方面再正確也不過了。希望你能全心吸收本書內容，並認眞聆聽搭配的CD，你將不只是與教材內容匆匆交會，而是實實在在學會了。

祝各位學習愉快。

Mark Hammons

CONTENTS

第三章 建立關係：閒聊 Creating a Relationship: Small Talk

第四章 轉入正題 Easing into Business

第五章 聚集焦點 Gaining Focus

第八章 與你的客戶或同事共事 Working with Your Customers or Colleagues

第九章 釐清問題 Sorting Out Problems

第十章 闡明議題 Clarifying Issues

取得聯絡
Making Contact

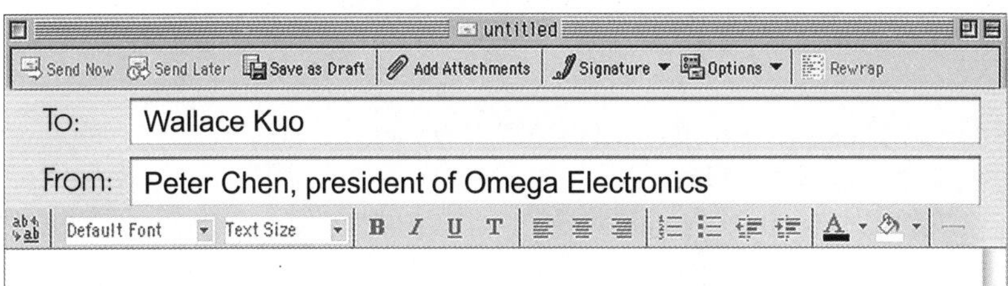

To: Wallace Kuo

From: Peter Chen, president of Omega Electronics

Wallace:

Please call Roland Kuhn of Ubertech about a sale of 1,000 memory sticks and 250 card readers. His number is 838-52295. Country code is 49. Berlin's city code is 30. He is expecting your call.

Thanks,
Peter

瓦勒斯：

請打電話給優博科技的洛藍・昆，討論一筆關於 1,000 張記憶卡和 250 部讀卡機的買賣。他的電話號碼是 838-52295 ，國碼是 49 ，柏林的市碼是 30 。他在等你的電話。

謝謝，
彼得

1 Biz 必通句型 Need-to-Know Phrases

CD I-02

1.1 自我介紹並要求與某人通話 Introducing Yourself and Asking for Someone

商務電訪時介紹自己並說明致電動機是非常基本的禮儀，下列三句用來簡單地介紹自己。

❶ Hi, this is (name) of (company) in (place).
您好，我是（地方）（公司）的（姓名）。
例 Hi, this is Wallace Kuo of Omega Electronics in Taiwan.
您好，我是台灣歐美嘉電子的瓦勒斯・郭。

❷ Hello, my name is ... from (company).
您好，我的名字叫……，我這裡是（公司）。
例 Hello, my name is Wallace Kuo from Omega Electronics.
您好，我的名字叫瓦勒斯・郭，我這裡是歐美嘉電子。

❸ Hello, I'm calling from (company) in (place).
您好，我是從（地方）（公司）打電話過來的。
例 Hello, I'm calling from Omega Electronics in Taiwan.
您好，我是從台灣歐美嘉電子打電話過來的。

this is ...（電話或 e-mail 中）我是……

下列五句用來說明自己要找誰。

❹ I'd like to speak with (contact name).
我想和（聯絡人的名字）說話。

例 I'd like to speak with Roland Kuhn.
我想和洛藍．昆說話。

❺ Could I have (contact name), extension (number), please?
能不能幫我接（聯絡人的名字），分機（號碼），麻煩你？

例 Could I have Roland Kuhn, extension 624, please?
能不能幫我接洛藍．昆，分機 624 ，麻煩你？

❻ I'm calling for (contact name).
我打電話來找（聯絡人名字）。

例 I'm calling for Roland Kuhn.
我打電話來找洛藍．昆。

❼ My name is ... I'm the (position) for (company).
我的名字叫……。我是（公司）的（職位）。

例 My name is Wallace Kuo. I'm the sales manager for Omega Electronics.
我的名字叫瓦勒斯．郭。我是歐美嘉電子的業務經理。

❽ Could you put me through to (contact name), please?
能不能請你幫我轉接（聯絡人姓名），麻煩你？

例 Could you put me through to Roland Kuhn, please?
能不能請你幫我轉接洛藍．昆，麻煩你？

Word List

contact [`kɑntækt] *n.* 聯絡人；聯絡；接觸
extension [ɪk`stɛnʃən] *n.* 電話分機；延伸
position [pə`zɪʃən] *n.* 職位；職務；位置
put through *phr. v.* 轉接（電話）

1.2 說明致電原因 Stating Reasons for a Call

❶ I'm calling in regard to ...

我打電話過來聯絡關於……。

例 I'm calling in regard to a discussion you had with Peter Chen.

我打電話過來聯絡關於您和彼得‧陳所做的一個討論。

❷ I'm calling about ...

我打電話過來聯絡有關……。

例 I'm calling about your interest in purchasing 1,000 LCD monitors.

我打電話過來聯絡有關您有意購買 1,000 台液晶顯示螢幕的事情。

❸ I'm calling to follow up on ...

我打電話過來對……做後續聯絡。

例 I'm calling to follow up on a conversation you had with Peter Chen at Berlin Consumer Electronics Trade Fair.

我打電話過來對您與彼得‧陳在柏林消費性電子展的談話做後續聯絡。

❹ I'm calling to discuss ...

我打電話過來討論……。

例 I'm calling to discuss your recent order that was placed on October 12.

我打電話過來討論您最近於十月十二號下的一筆訂單。

state [stet] *v.* 說明；陳述

in regard to 關於

LCD *n.* 液晶螢幕（liquid crystal display [`lɪkwɪd `krɪstḷ dɪs͵ple] 的縮寫）

monitor [`mɑnətɚ] *n.* 監視器

follow up *phr. v.* 做後續聯絡

place [ples] *v.* 下訂單；安置

❺ I'm phoning on behalf of (name).

我代表（姓名）打這通電話。

例 I'm phoning on behalf of Peter Chen, president of Omega Electronics.

我代表歐美嘉電子的總裁彼得．陳打這通電話。

❻ I believe you spoke with (name) about ...

我相信您曾和（姓名）談論有關……。

例 I believe you spoke with Peter Chen about the purchase of computer mice and other accessories.

我相信您曾和彼得．陳談論有關購買電腦滑鼠和其他配件的事宜。

❼ I understand you had a discussion with (person) regarding ...

我知道您曾和（人）討論過關於……的事。

例 I understand you had a discussion with Peter Chen regarding the purchase of computer keyboards and LCDs.

我知道您曾和彼得．陳討論過關於購買電腦鍵盤與液晶顯示螢幕的事。

❽ Mr./Ms. (name) asked me to call you about ...

（姓名）先生／小姐要我打電話與您聯絡有關……。

例 Mr. Peter Chen asked me to call you about your recent order. He said you had some questions you needed help with.

彼得．陳先生要我打電話與您聯絡有關您最近所下的訂單。他說您有一些疑問需要幫忙。

Word List

on behalf of sb. 代表某人（= on sb.'s behalf [bɪˋhæf]）

mice [maɪs] *n.* 滑鼠；鼠（mouse 的複數）

accessory [ækˋsɛsərɪ] *n.* 附件；配件

2 實戰會話 Show Time

2.1 Dialogue

CD I-03

Wallace Kuo calls Roland Kuhn to talk about the details of Ubertech's first order.

Receptionist 1: Ubertech.

Wallace: Hi, this is Wallace Kuo of Omega Electronics in Taiwan. I'd like to speak with Roland Kuhn.

Receptionist 1: I'll put you through to Purchasing. Please hold.

Receptionist 2 Purchasing. How can I help you?

Wallace: Hello, this is Wallace Kuo. I'm calling for Mr. Roland Kuhn.

Receptionist 2 Let me transfer you to Mr. Kuhn's secretary. Please hold.

Wallace: Thank you.

Roland's secretary: Roland Kuhn's office. How can I assist you?

Wallace: Hi, this is Wallace Kuo of Omega Electronics in Taiwan. Is Mr. Kuhn in?

Roland's secretary: Yes, he is. I'll put you through.

Roland: Hello, Roland Kuhn here.

Wallace: My name is Wallace Kuo. I'm the sales manager for Omega Electronics in Taiwan.

譯文

瓦勒斯．郭打電話給洛藍．昆討論有關優博科技第一張訂單的細節。

總機 1：　優博科技。

瓦勒斯：　您好，我是台灣歐美嘉電子的瓦勒斯．郭。我想和洛藍．昆說話。

總機 1：　我幫您轉到採購部。請稍等。

總機 2：　採購部，我能提供您什麼協助？

瓦勒斯：　您好，我是瓦勒斯．郭。我打電話過來找洛藍．昆先生。

總機 2：　我幫您轉給昆先生的秘書。請稍等。

瓦勒斯：　謝謝。

洛藍的秘書：洛藍．昆的辦公室。我能幫您做什麼嗎？

瓦勒斯：　您好，我是台灣歐美嘉電子的瓦勒斯．郭。昆先生在嗎？

洛藍的秘書：是的，他在。我幫您轉過去。

洛藍：　您好，我是洛藍．昆。

瓦勒斯：　我的名字叫瓦勒斯．郭。我是台灣歐美嘉電子的業務經理。

Word List

receptionist [rɪ`sɛpʃənɪst] *n.* 櫃檯人員；接待人員
transfer [træns`fɝ] *v.* 轉移；轉換；調動
assist [ə`sɪst] *v.* 幫助；協助

2.2 Dialogue

Wallace continues his discussion with Roland and introduces the reason for his call.

Roland: Hello, Mr. Kuo. How can I help you?

Wallace: I'm calling to follow up on a conversation you had with Peter Chen at the Hannover Computer Show.

Roland: Yes, I remember.

Wallace: I understand you had a discussion regarding the purchase of memory sticks and card readers.

Roland: Hmm. I wasn't expecting your call so soon. Let me get my notes.

Wallace: No problem.

Roland: Right. I have it right here in front of me. We discussed an order of 1,000 memory sticks and 250 card readers.

Wallace: Yes, that's what Mr. Chen told me. There are a number of issues we need to discuss regarding your purchase.

瓦勒斯繼續他與洛藍的討論並提出他打這通電話的原因。

洛藍：　哈囉，郭先生。我能幫你什麼忙嗎？

瓦勒斯：我打電話過來對您和彼得．陳在漢諾威電腦展的談話做後續聯絡。

洛藍：　是的，我記得。

瓦勒斯：我知道你們曾討論過關於購買記憶卡與讀卡機的事。

洛藍：　嗯唔。我沒預期你這麼快就打電話來。讓我拿一下我的筆記。

瓦勒斯：沒問題。

洛藍：　好了，我拿到了，就在我面前。我們討論了一筆 1,000 張記憶卡和 250 部讀卡機的訂單。

瓦勒斯：是的，陳先生是這麼告訴我的。關於您的訂購，有幾個問題我們需要討論一下。

expect [ɪk`spɛkt] *v.* 預期；期待

3 Biz 加分句型 Nice-to-Know Phrases

3.1 釐清名稱 Getting a Name Right

❶ **Could you repeat that please?**（當你沒聽清楚時）
可以請您重複一遍嗎？

例 I didn't catch what you just said. Could you repeat that please?
我沒聽清楚您剛才講的。可以請您重複一遍嗎？

❷ **I'm sorry ... How do you pronounce it?**（當你不確定正確發音時）
對不起……。這該怎麼發音？

例 I'm sorry. I couldn't hear that clearly. How do you pronounce it?
對不起，我沒有聽清楚。應該怎麼發音？

❸ **I'm sorry. How do you spell that?**（當你不確定拼法時）
對不起，那該怎麼拼？

例 I'm sorry. How do you spell that? I couldn't hear you over the traffic noise.
對不起，那該怎麼拼？車聲很吵我沒辦法聽清楚你說的話。

❹ **That's the information I was given. What is the correct spelling of your name?**（當你手上的資料有誤時）
我拿到的資料是那樣的。您的名字正確的拼法應該是？

例 I apologize for getting your name wrong. That's the information I was given. What is the correct spelling of your name?
很抱歉將您的名字弄錯了，我拿到的資料是那樣的。您的大名正確拼法應該是？

Word List

catch [kætʃ] *v.* 聽清楚；理解
apologize [əˋpɑlə͵dʒaɪz] *v.* 道歉（apologize for V-ing/N. 爲……致歉）

3.2 撥對分機號碼 Getting an Extension Number Right

❶ **I'm sorry. Do you have the extension number for (name)?**（當你撥錯分機時，用來詢問正確號碼）

對不起，你有（人名）的分機號碼嗎？

例 I'm sorry. Do you have the extension number for Sylvia Huang?

對不起，你有絲薇亞．黃的分機號碼嗎？

❷ **I'm calling for (name) and I seem to have the wrong extension number.**（當你發現自己撥錯分機時）

我打過來找（人名），不過我似乎打錯分機號碼了。

例 I'm calling for Timothy Chao and I seem to have the wrong extension number.

我打過來找提莫西．趙，不過我似乎打錯分機號碼了。

❸ **Could I please have (name)'s extension?**（詢問正確的分機號碼）

可不可以給我（人名）的分機號碼？

例 Could I please have Hans Greenman's extension?

可不可以給我漢斯．格林門的分機號碼？

❹ **Does (name) have his/her own extension?**（不確定要找的人是否有專用分機時）

（人名）有他／她專屬的分機號碼嗎？

例 Does David have his own extension number, or does he share a phone with his colleagues?

大衛有沒有他專屬的分機號碼，還是和他的同事共用一支電話？

小心陷阱

☹ 錯誤用法

Hi, **I am** Wallace Kuo. I **call from** Taiwan **of** Omega Electronics.

您好，我是瓦勒斯・郭。我是從台灣歐美嘉電子打過來的。

☺ 正確用法：

Hi, **this is** Wallace Kuo. I**'m calling from** Omega Electronics **in** Taiwan.

您好，我是瓦勒斯・郭。我是從台灣歐美嘉電子打過來的。

文化小叮嚀

European businesspeople, like European consumers, are not swayed by emotional appeals associated with new products. They are more likely to be motivated by logic and well-defined product characteristics. Despite your phone-based friendly relationship with your customer, it is best to present specific product attributes when selling on the phone.

歐洲的商務人士，就像歐洲的消費者，不會因為新產品的情緒號召而動搖。他們的購買慾比較可能被理性和明確的產品特性所激發。儘管你和顧客的「電話」關係不錯，打電話推銷時最好還是提出產品的具體特性。

Word List

be swayed by ... 被……影響

appeal [ə`pil] *n.* 吸引力

associate [ə`soʃɪˌet] *v.* 有關；聯想

motivate [`motəˌvet] *v.* 給……動機；激發

logic [`lɑdʒɪk] *n.* 邏輯；道理

well-defined [`wɛl `dɪfaɪnd] *adj.*（定義）明確的

characteristic [ˌkærɪktə`rɪstɪk] *n.* 特徵；特性

specific [spɪ`sɪfɪk] *adj.* 明確的；特定的

attribute [`ætrɪˌbjut] *n.* 特性；特質

4 實戰演練 Practice Exercises

I 請為下列三題選出最適本章的中文譯義。

❶ put ... through

(A) 為……引見 (B) 替……轉告 (C) 為……轉接

❷ in regard to ...

(A) 向……問候致意 (B) 關於…… (C) 當作……

❸ follow up on ...

(A) 緊跟著…… (B) 針對……追蹤聯絡 (C) 接著做……

II 請根據你聽到的內容為下列兩題選出正確解答。

❶ Who is calling Scott Enterprises?

(A) David Walker.

(B) Scott Jacobsen.

(C) David Anderson.

❷ What will happen next?

(A) Mr. Walker will call Scott Enterprises.

(B) Mr. Walker will talk to Mr. Jacobsen.

(C) Mr. Jacobsen will call Next Electronics.

III 幾番轉接、一陣等待之後，你終於和想找的客戶聯絡上了。這是你第一次打電話給這位客戶，所以需要簡短地介紹一下自己並說明致電動機。實際打電話之前，利用下列詞語模擬情境，事先準備好要講的話吧：

this is	from/of/in	speak with
in regard to	express interest in	

＊解答請見 216 頁

接聽來電
Answering a Call

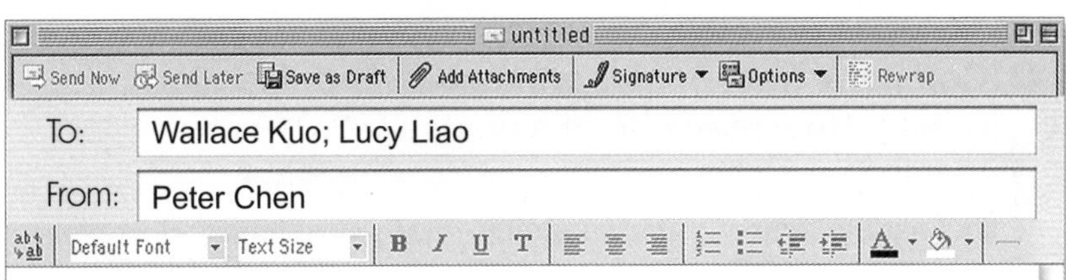

Lucy and Wallace:

I've had some complaints from customers about our phone manners. It seems that some customers prefer formal, rather than informal, manners. Please ensure that you sound professional on the phone.

Thanks,
Peter
President
Omega Electronics, Taiwan

露西和瓦勒斯：

我從客戶那邊接到一些關於我們電話禮儀的抱怨。看來有些客戶比較喜歡正式的，而非非正式的，禮儀。請確定你們在講電話的時候聽起來很專業。

謝謝，
彼得
台灣歐美嘉電子總裁

1 Biz 必通句型 Need-to-Know Phrases

1.1 接聽電話 Answering a Call

CD I-06

電話接通後答話者的回應方式非常重要，專業、親切的態度會使來電者對公司留下深刻良好的印象，用下列八句來建立專業的第一「耳」印象吧。

❶ (Company name), (department/division/section), (name). How may I be of assistance?

（公司名稱），（部門），（姓名）。我能提供什麼協助嗎？

例 Fast Systems, sales department, Hans Greenman. How may I be of assistance?

飛速特系統，銷售部，漢斯．格林門。我能提供什麼協助嗎？

❷ Good morning/afternoon/evening/day. (Company/department name), how may/can I assist you?

早／午／晚／日安，（公司／部門名稱）。我能幫您做什麼嗎？

例 Good morning. Universal Marketing. How can I assist you?

早安，寰宇行銷。我能幫您做什麼嗎？

❸ (Name), (company/department name). How may/can I help you?

（姓名），（公司／部門名稱）。我能幫您什麼忙嗎？

例 Tina Chen, V3 Global Communications. How may I help you?

蒂娜．陳，V3 全球通訊。我能幫您什麼忙嗎？

Word List

department [dɪˋpɑrtmənt] *n.*（行政、企業的）司、局、部、處；（學校的）系、科

division [dəˋvɪʒən] *n.*（公司、機關的）部門、處、課；分區；分隊

section [ˋsɛkʃən] *n.*（公司、機關的）部門、處、科、股、組

assistance [əˋsɪstəns] *n.* 援助；幫助（be of assistance 提供協助）

❹ (Name). What may/can I do for you, today?

（姓名）。今天有什麼我可以為您服務的嗎？

例 Timothy Chao. What may I do for you, today?

提莫西．趙。今天有什麼我可以為您服務的嗎？

❺ Hello, this is (name) of (company/department name).

您好，我是（公司／部門名稱）的（姓名）。

例 Hello, this is Lucy Liao of Omega Electronics in Taiwan.

您好，我是台灣歐美嘉電子的露西．廖。

❻ (Company/department name). How may/can I direct your call?

（公司／部門名稱）。請問我該如何為您轉接？

例 Handi Resources. How can I direct your call?

翰迪資源。請問我該如何為您轉接？

❼ (Company name), (country name). How may I help you?

（國名）（公司名稱）。我能幫您什麼忙嗎？

例 Transplanet Airlines, Taiwan. How may I help you?

台灣環球航空。我能幫您什麼忙嗎？

❽ Hello, (position), (name) speaking.

您好，我是（職位）（姓名）。

例 Hello, production manager, Sylvia Huang speaking.

您好，我是生產經理絲薇亞．黃。

Word List

direct [də`rɛkt] *v.*（電話）轉接；指示；指導

position [pə`zɪʃən] *n.* 職務；職位；工作

production [prə`dʌkʃən] *n.* 生產；製造

1.2 取得基本資料與轉接電話 Obtaining Key Information and Directing a Call

稱職的接聽者有一項相當重要的任務——過濾來電；用下列四句詢問來電者的身分及致電動機，以排除擾人的電話。

❶ This is (company/department name). May I ask who is calling?
這裡是（公司／部門名稱）。請問是哪位打來的？

例 This is the customer service center. May I ask who is calling?
這裡是顧客服務中心。請問是哪位打來的？

❷ Who would you like to speak with, (caller name)?
請問您要找誰，（來電者姓名）？

例 Who would you like to speak with, Mr. Smith?
請問您要找誰，史密斯先生？

❸ May I ask you, (caller name), what your call is in regard to?
（來電者姓名），能請問您這通電話是關於什麼事情嗎？

例 May I ask you, Mr. Smith, what your call is in regard to?
史密斯先生，能請問您這通電話是關於什麼事情嗎？

❹ May I ask what your call concerns, (caller name)?
我能請問您這通電話是有關何事嗎，（來電者姓名）？

例 May I ask what your call concerns, Mr. Smith?
我能請問您這通電話是有關何事嗎，史密斯先生？

Word List

obtain [əb`ten] *v.* 獲得；取得
concern [kən`sɝn] *v.* 與……有關；使……擔心

確定並非無謂的來電後，用下列四句將電話轉給來電者想找的人聽。

❺ Please hold while I direct you to our (position, name).

請稍等，我幫您轉給我們的（職位，姓名）。

例 Please hold while I direct you to our sales manager, Wallace Kuo.

請稍等，我幫您轉給我們的業務經理，瓦勒斯．郭。

❻ Let me transfer you to (name/department/division/section). Please hold.

我幫您轉接（姓名／部門）。請稍等。

例 Let me transfer you to the editorial department. Please hold.

我幫您轉接編輯部。請稍等。

❼ Please wait while I check to see if (name) is in.

請稍待，我看一下（姓名）是否在辦公室。

例 Please wait while I check to see if Mr. Greenman is in.

請稍待，我看一下格林門先生是否在辦公室。

❽ Let me transfer you to (name) right away, Mr./Ms. (name).

我馬上幫您轉接（姓名），（姓名）先生／小姐。

例 Let me transfer you to Ms. Huang right away, Mr. Toffler.

我馬上幫您轉接黃小姐，陶福勒先生。

editorial [ˌɛdəˋtorɪəl] *adj.* 編輯（上）的；社論（式）的

check to see if ... 查一下看看是否……

2 實戰會話 Show Time

CD I-07

2.1 Dialogue

Lucy Liao receives a call asking to talk to Peter Chen at Omega Electronics.

Lucy: Omega Electronics, Taiwan. How may I help you?

Caller: Is Peter in? I spoke with him about purchasing 1,000 memory sticks and 250 card readers.

Lucy: Let me transfer you to Wallace Kuo, our sales manager. Please hold.

Wallace: Hello, sales manager, Wallace Kuo speaking.

Lucy Liao needs to get in touch with Marie Arndt at Ubertech to discuss the payment schedule.

Receptionist: Ubertech. How may I direct your call?

Lucy: I'd like to speak with Marie Arndt in accounting.

Receptionist: Please hold.

Female Voice: Ubertech, accounting. How may I be of assistance?

Lucy: Could I have Marie Arndt, please?

Female Voice: May I ask who is calling?

Lucy: Lucy Liao of Omega Electronics in Taiwan.

Female Voice: Ms. Liao, let me transfer you to Ms. Arndt. Please hold.

Marie: Hello, accounting, Marie Arndt speaking.

譯文

露西．廖接到一通電話要求和歐美嘉電子的彼得．陳說話。

露西：　台灣歐美嘉電子。我能幫您什麼忙嗎？

來電者：彼得在嗎？我和他談過有關購買 1,000 張記憶卡和 250 部讀卡機的事。

露西：　我幫您轉接瓦勒斯．郭，我們的業務經理。請稍等。

瓦勒斯：您好，我是業務經理瓦勒斯．郭。

露西．廖需要和優博科技的瑪莉．阿恩特聯絡討論付款時程。

總機：　優博科技。請問我該如何為您轉接？

露西：　我想和會計部的瑪莉．阿恩特通話。

總機：　請稍等。

女聲：　優博科技，會計部。我能提供什麼協助嗎？

露西：　能不能幫我接瑪莉．阿恩特，麻煩妳？

女聲：　請問是哪位打來的？

露西：　台灣歐美嘉電子的露西．廖。

女聲：　廖小姐，我幫您轉接阿恩特小姐。請稍等。

瑪莉：　您好，我是會計部的瑪莉．阿恩特。

2.2 Dialogue

Lucy Liao is answering the phone today.

Lucy: Good morning. Omega Electronics. How can I assist you?

Caller: Wallace Kuo, please.

Lucy: Could I have your name, please?

Caller: Mike Smith.

(Response 1)

Lucy: May I ask you, Mr. Smith, what your call is regarding?

Mike: Yes, I'm interested in purchasing some memory sticks.

Lucy: Please hold while I direct you to our sales department.

(Response 2)

Lucy: May I ask what your call concerns, Mr. Smith?

Mike: Yes, I've been waiting for Wallace Kuo to call me back.

Lucy: Please wait while I check to see if Mr. Kuo is in.

Lucy: Wallace, there is a Mike Smith calling for you. He says he's been waiting for you to call him.

Wallace: Put him through.

Lucy: Mr. Smith, let me transfer you to Mr. Kuo right away.

Mike: Thanks.

Wallace: Sorry for not calling you sooner, Mr. Smith. I have those prices right here.

譯文

露西・廖今天負責接聽電話。

露西：　早安。歐美嘉電子。我能幫您做什麼嗎？

來電者：請接瓦勒斯・郭。

露西：　可以請問您是哪位嗎？

來電者：麥可・史密斯。

（回應一）

露西：　史密斯先生，能請問您這通電話是關於什麼事情嗎？

麥可：　是的，我想購買一些記憶卡。

露西：　請稍等，我幫您轉給我們的業務部。

（回應二）

露西：　我能請問您這通電話關於何事嗎，史密斯先生？

麥可：　是，我一直在等瓦勒斯・郭回電給我。

露西：　請稍待，我看一下郭先生是否在辦公室。

露西：　瓦勒斯，有位麥可・史密斯打電話找你。他說他一直在等你打電話給他。

瓦勒斯：把他的電話接過來。

露西：　史密斯先生，我馬上幫您轉接郭先生。

麥可：　謝謝。

瓦勒斯：抱歉沒能早點回電給您，史密斯先生。我手邊現在有價目表。

3 Biz 加分句型 Nice-to-Know Phrases

3.1 當你聽不到／聽不懂時 When You Can't Hear/Understand

❶ I'm sorry, (name). Could you repeat that please?
（當你沒聽清楚，希望對方重述時）
對不起，（姓名）。能不能請您重複一遍？

例 I'm sorry, Hans, the reception is not good. Could you repeat that please?
對不起，漢斯，收訊不太好。能不能請你重複一遍？

❷ I'm sorry, (name). I'll have to ask you to repeat that.
（要求對方重述）
對不起，（姓名）。我必須請您重複一遍。

例 I'm sorry, Kearny. I'll have to ask you to repeat that.
對不起，柯尼。我必須請你重複一遍。

❸ I'm sorry, (name). Could you speak more slowly please?（當對方講話速度太快時）
對不起，（姓名）。能不能請您說慢一點？

例 I'm sorry, Bernard. Could you speak more slowly please?
對不起，伯納。能不能請你說慢一點？

❹ Sorry, (name). I didn't quite understand what you said.（當你聽不懂對方的意思時）
抱歉，（姓名）。我不太懂您剛才說的。

例 Sorry, Mark. I didn't quite understand what you said. Could you please repeat it again?
抱歉，馬克。我不太懂你剛才說的。能不能請你再重複一遍？

Word List

reception [rɪˋsɛpʃən] *n.*（影音等訊息的）接收；接收品質；接收效果

3.2 當轉接未成功時 When Directing the Call Is Unsuccessful

❶ I'm very sorry, (caller name), the call didn't go through.（當電話沒接通轉回時）

非常抱歉，（來電者姓名），電話沒有接通。

例 I'm very sorry, Mr. Simpson, the call didn't go through. Let me try to transfer you again.

非常抱歉，辛普森先生，電話沒有接通。讓我再試著幫您轉一次。

❷ I'm very sorry, (caller name). Let me put you through again.（再次代為轉接）

非常抱歉，（來電者姓名）。我再幫您轉一次。

例 I'm very sorry, Ms. Chao. Let me put you through again.

非常抱歉，趙小姐。我再幫妳轉一次。

❸ I apologize, (caller name). Let me try that again.（當你按錯分機號碼時）

對不起，（來電者姓名）。讓我再試一次。

例 I apologize, Mr. Kuhn. Let me try that again.

對不起，昆先生。讓我再試一次。

❹ I'm sorry, (name) seems to be on the other line.（當被找的人忙線中時）

抱歉，（姓名）似乎在另一條線上。

例 I'm sorry, Mr. Chen seems to be on the other line. Would you like to hold?

抱歉，陳先生似乎在另一條線上。您要等待嗎？

go through *phr. v.*（電話）接通；（法案、提議等）通過；經歷；檢視

小心陷阱

☹ 錯誤用法

Wallace, there is **the** Ms. Smith calling for you. She says **she's waiting you** to call **him**.

瓦勒斯，有位史密斯小姐打電話找你。她說她一直在等你打電話給她。

☺ 正確用法

Wallace, there is **a** Ms. Smith calling for you. She says **she's been waiting for you** to call **her**.

瓦勒斯，有位史密斯小姐打電話找你。她說她一直在等你打電話給她。

文化小叮嚀

When dealing with most female North Americans, it is important that you use Ms. before a woman's family name until your relationship becomes less formal or until the woman tells you otherwise. Both Mrs. and Miss are considered slightly rude by some Western women.

在和大多數的北美洲女性應對時，除非你們已經比較熟或是她們直接告訴你該如何稱呼她們，否則在她們的姓氏之前冠上 Ms. 很重要。有些西方女性認為 Mrs.（太太）和 Miss（未婚小姐）這兩種稱謂不太禮貌。

deal with *phr. v.* 應付；處理

Ms. [mɪz] *n.* 女士（這個稱謂避免提及婚姻狀況，是比較有禮貌的說法；近似中文裡常禮貌通稱女性為「小姐」）

otherwise [\`ʌðɚˏwaɪz] *adv.* 以其他方式；否則

be considered N./Adj. 被認爲是……

slightly [\`slaɪtlɪ] *adv.* 輕微地；稍微地

rude [rud] *adj.* 無禮的；粗魯的

4 實戰演練 Practice Exercises

I 請為下列三題選出最適本章的中文譯義。

❶ direct you to ...

(A) 指引你到…… (B) 將你轉接到…… (C) 命令你去……

❷ transfer you to ...

(A) 把你調到…… (B) 幫你換到…… (C) 將你轉接到……

❸ go through

(A) 通過 (B) 經歷 (C) 接通

II 請根據你聽到的內容為下列兩題選出正確解答。

❶ Which company is the caller from?

(A) Speedy Systems.

(B) Exports Department.

(C) Omega Electronics.

❷ Where will the phone call be directed?

(A) To Ms. Gray at Omega Electronics.

(B) To Ms. Gray in the Imports Department.

(C) To Ms. Gray in the Exports Department.

III 電話響了，有人要找你的同事，而他／她剛好離開座位，所以你幫忙接聽電話。利用下列詞語寫一短篇回應模擬一下實境吧。

out of the office　　take a message　　will be back

call you back

＊解答請見 218 頁

建立關係：閒聊

Creating a Relationship: Small Talk

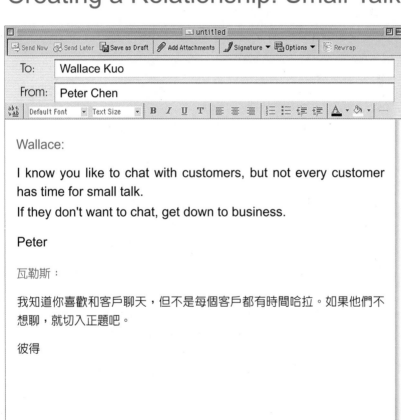

untitled

Send Now | Send Later | Save as Draft | Add Attachments | Signature | Options | Rewrap

To: Wallace Kuo

From: Peter Chen

Default Font | Text Size

Wallace:

I know you like to chat with customers, but not every customer has time for small talk.
If they don't want to chat, get down to business.

Peter

瓦勒斯：

我知道你喜歡和客戶聊天，但不是每個客戶都有時間哈拉。如果他們不想聊，就切入正題吧。

彼得

1 Biz 必通句型 Need-to-Know Phrases

CD I-10

1.1 聊非正事話題 Introducing Non-Business Topics

❶ **Hello, ... How is the weather in ...?**
哈囉，……。……的天氣如何？
例 Hello, Roland. How's the weather in Berlin?
哈囉，洛藍。柏林的天氣如何？

❷ **..., are you by any chance a ... fan?**
……，你會不會碰巧是個……迷？
例 Roland, are you by any chance a football fan?
洛藍，你會不會碰巧是個足球迷？

❸ **..., did I tell you I ... last weekend?**
……，我有沒有跟你說過我上週末……？
例 Ms. Arndt, did I tell you I went hiking last weekend?
阿恩特小姐，我有沒有跟妳說過我上週末去登山健行？

❹ **..., did I tell you what happened to me the other day when I ...?**
……，我有沒有跟你說幾天前我……的時候發生的事？
例 Marie, did I tell you what happened to me the other day when I was driving home from work?
瑪莉，我有沒有跟妳說幾天前我下班開車回家的時候發生的事？

Word List

topic [`tɑpɪk] *n.* 話題；標題；主題
by any chance（用於問句中）也許；碰巧
the other day 不久前的某一天（與過去式連用）

❺ ..., do you know what happened to me ...?
……，你知道……我發生了什麼事嗎？

例 Mr. Kuhn, do you know what happened to me last week?
昆先生，你知道上個禮拜我發生了什麼事嗎？

❻ ..., I've got a funny (joke/story) to tell you.
……，我有個有趣的（笑話／故事）要告訴你。

例 Roland, I've got a funny story to tell you.
洛藍，我有個有趣的故事要告訴你。

❼ ..., I was reading (the news story/a book/an article) (when) and it said that ...
……，我（何時）在看（新聞報導／一本書／一篇文章），上面說……。

例 Roland, I was reading an article yesterday and it said that German movies are very popular in Europe right now.
洛藍，我昨天在看一篇文章，上面說德國電影現在在歐洲非常受歡迎。

❽ ..., I was talking to a friend of mine, and he/she said that ...
……，我才跟我一位朋友在聊，他／她說……。

例 Marie, I was talking to a friend of mine, and he said that I should take a holiday in Switzerland.
瑪莉，我才跟我一位朋友在聊，他說我應該休假到瑞士玩。

Word List

take a holiday 休假
Switzerland [ˋswɪtsɚlənd] *n.* 瑞士

1.2 談論景氣 Talking About the Business Climate

和客戶交換市場訊息有可能爲日後帶來無限商機。

❶ ..., how has business been?

……，最近生意如何？

例 Marie, how has business been?

瑪莉，最近生意如何？

❷ ..., how is the economy in (country/region/city) these days?

……，近來（國家／地區／城市）的經濟怎麼樣？

例 Lucy, how is the economy in Taiwan these days?

露西，近來台灣的經濟怎麼樣？

❸ How are things going in (country/region/city)?

（國家／地區／城市）的情況怎麼樣？

例 How are things going in Munich?

慕尼黑的情況怎麼樣？

❹ ..., what's ... like in ...?

……，……的……狀況如何？

例 Marie, what's the business climate like in Germany?

瑪莉，德國的景氣狀況如何？

Word List

climate [ˋklaɪmɪt] *n.* 氣候；趨勢；風尚
economy [ɪˋkɑnəmi] *n.* 經濟；節約
region [ˋriʤən] *n.* 地區；領域
these days 近來；這一陣子
Munich [ˋmjunɪk] *n.*（德國）慕尼黑

❺ How have ... been lately?

最近……如何？

例 Marie, how have <u>sales</u> been lately?

瑪莉，最近銷量如何？

❻ Business in (country/region/city) is (great/not too bad/slow) ...

（國家／地區／城市）的景氣……（好極了／還算不錯／冷清）。

例 Business in Taiwan is not too bad right now.

台灣的景氣目前還算不錯。

❼ Business is ... Our sales (are <u>stable</u>/have increased/have <u>dropped off</u>) (a little/<u>considerably</u>/<u>substantially</u>) over ...

生意……。我們的銷量在……期間（平穩／增加了／下降了）（一點點／頗多／非常多）。

例 Business is great. Our sales have increased substantially over the last month.

生意很好。我們的銷量上個月增加了非常多。

❽ What is the (<u>forecast</u>/<u>projection</u>) for the economy in ... over the next few (weeks/months)?

未來幾（週／月）間……的經濟（預測／預估）情況如何？

例 Marie, what is the projection for the economy in Taiwan over the next few months?

瑪莉，未來幾個月台灣的經濟預估情況如何？

Word List

sales [selz] *n.*（複數形）銷售量；業務部門
stable [\`stebḷ] *adj.* 穩定的
drop off *phr. v.* 減少；下降
considerably [kən\`sɪdərəblɪ] *adv.* 相當；頗
substantially [səb\`stænʃəlɪ] *adv.* 大大地；大量地
forecast [\`for͵kæst] *n./v.* 預測；預報
projection [prə\`dʒɛkʃən] *n.* 預估；推斷；（影像的）投射

2 實戰會話 Show Time

CD I-11

2.1 Dialogue

Wallace has established a good relationship with Roland. He's calling to talk about a new order. But before he gets down to business, he chats with Roland.

Roland: Hi, Wallace. How are you?

Wallace: Hello, Roland. How's the weather in Berlin?

Roland: Not too bad. It's a little cold right now. The fall is always cold.

Wallace: It's still summer here. Did I tell you I went hiking last weekend?

Roland: Hiking? No. Where did you go?

Wallace: Just up to the mountains around the city. Roland, I've got a funny story to tell you.

Roland: Good. I can always use a good laugh.

Wallace: When I was hiking, my wife found a ring. It was covered with dirt. When we returned home, she washed it. Believe it or not, it was a ring she lost as a little girl hiking on the same trail.

Roland: Unbelievable!

Wallace: Unbelievable. I was talking to a friend of mine, and he said that a similar thing happened to his mother when he was in university.

譯文

瓦勒斯已經和洛藍建立了良好的關係。他打電話要談一筆新的訂單。但在切入正題之前，他先和洛藍聊一下天。

洛藍：　嗨，瓦勒斯。你好嗎？

瓦勒斯：哈囉，洛藍。柏林的天氣如何？

洛藍：　還不錯。現在有一點冷。秋天總是會冷。

瓦勒斯：我這裡還是夏天。我有沒有跟你說過我上週末去登山健行？

洛藍：　登山健行？沒有。你去了哪裡？

瓦勒斯：只是城市附近的山上。洛藍，我有個有趣的故事要告訴你。

洛藍：　太好了。我一向都需要好好地笑一下。

瓦勒斯：我在健行的時候，我太太發現了一只戒指。上面都是泥巴。我們回到家之後，她把它洗乾淨。信不信由你，那是她小時候爬同一條山路時弄丟的戒指。

洛藍：　難以置信！

瓦勒斯：很難令人相信。我才跟我一位朋友在聊，他說在他讀大學的時候，類似的事情曾發生在他媽媽身上。

Word List

establish a relationship with ... 與……建立關係
get down to business 開始辦正事
could use something（口語）非常需要某事物
dirt [dɝt] *n.* 泥；土；灰塵
trail [trel] *n.*（山間郊野的）小道

2.2 Dialogue

Lucy starts a conversation with Marie about the economy in Germany.

Lucy: Marie, how has business been?

Marie: Business is great. Our sales have increased substantially over the last month. Lucy, how is the economy in Taiwan these days?

Lucy: Business in Taiwan is not too bad right now, even though we've had a bit of a slowdown. Marie, what is the projection for the German economy over the next few months?

Marie: We expect things will remain stable for a while. We are hoping that the new products next year will bump us up again. What is the long-term forecast for Taiwan's economy?

Lucy: We expect that our declining dollar is going to be good for the export business over the next 6 months.

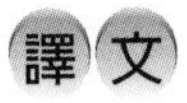
譯文

露西和瑪莉開始談論起德國的經濟。

露西：瑪莉，最近生意如何？

瑪莉：生意好極了。我們的銷量上個月增加了非常多。露西，近來台灣的經濟怎麼樣？

露西：台灣的景氣目前還算不錯，雖然稍微有一點減緩。瑪莉，未來幾個月德國的經濟預估情況如何？

瑪莉：我們預計情況將會暫時維持穩定。我們希望明年的新產品能再次拉抬我們的銷售業績。台灣經濟的長期預測如何？

露西：我們期望接下來的六個月台幣走弱能有助出口業務。

Word List

start a conversation with sb. 與某人開始交談
slowdown [`slo͵daʊn] *n.* 減速；減緩
remain [rɪ`men] *v.* 保持；停留；繼續存在
a while 一段時間；一陣子
bump up *phr. v.*（數目）突然大增；增加；提高
long-term [`lɔŋ͵tɝm] *adj.* 長期的
declining [dɪ`klaɪnɪŋ] *adj.* 減少的；下降的；衰退的
export [`ɛksport] *n.* 出口；輸出品

3 Biz 加分句型 Nice-to-Know Phrases

CD I-12

3.1 當你誤解問題時 When You Misunderstood the Question

❶ **I'm sorry. I thought ...**
對不起。我以為……。

例 I'm sorry. I thought you were asking me about the short-term forecast for the economy.
對不起。我以為你在問我經濟的短期預測。

❷ **Of course, you meant ... I misunderstood your question.**
當然，你是指……。我誤解你的問題了。

例 Of course, you meant, how are sales? I misunderstood your question.
當然，你是指銷量如何？我誤解你的問題了。

❸ **Oh, I see. You wanted to know about ...**
喔，我懂了。你想知道……。

例 Oh, I see. You wanted to know about our maximum discount if you place an order for 30,000 units.
喔，我懂了。你想知道如果你下一張三萬組的訂單，我們最大的折扣是多少。

❹ **I understand now. You were talking about ...**
我現在懂了。你在說……。

例 I understand now. You were talking about the discount we offer for cash payments.
我現在懂了。你在說我們對現金付款所提供的折扣。

Word List

short-term [`ʃɔrt `tɝm] *adj.* 短期的
maximum [`mæksəməm] *n.* 最大值；最高限度
discount [`dɪskaʊnt] *n.* 折扣；*v.* 打折
place an order (for sth.) 下訂單（訂購某物）
unit [`junɪt] *n.* 一組；單位
payment [`pemənt] *n.* [C] 支付的款項；[U] 付款（行爲）

3.2 當你不知道答案時 When You Don't Know the Answer

❶ I'm not sure. Let me ... I'll have the answer for you next time.（必須向外求援時）

我不確定。讓我……。下次我會給你答案。

例 I'm not sure. Let me ask our sales department. I'll have the answer for you next time.

我不確定。讓我問一下我們的業務部。下次我會給你答案。

❷ Off the top of my head, I really don't know ...（無法立即答覆時）

突然要我講，我真的不知道……。

例 Off the top of my head, I really don't know when we can get your order shipped.

突然要我講，我真的不知道我們什麼時候能運送你的貨。

❸ Let me ask ... Please hold for a minute.（能立刻找出解答時）

讓我問一下……。請稍待一下。

例 Let me ask our shipping manager. Please hold for a minute.

讓我問一下我們的出貨經理。請稍待一下。

❹ Do you need to know ... right now?（想知道客戶是否馬上就要答案時）

你需要立刻知道……嗎？

例 Do you need to know the delivery date right now?

你需要立刻知道交貨日期嗎？

Word List

off the top of my head 突然要我講；馬上要我說的話（表示接下來說的話未經思索、沒有準備）

get sth. shipped 運送某物（get 加受詞後接形容詞或過去分詞，表示造成、使役……）

shipping [`ʃɪpɪŋ] *n.* 運送；出貨

delivery [dɪ`lɪvərɪ] *n.* 交貨；遞送

小心陷阱

☹ 錯誤用法

Sales **has been** substantially **increase in** last few months.

銷量在過去幾個月大幅增加。

☺ 正確用法

Sales **have** substantially **increased over the** last few months.

銷量在過去幾個月大幅增加。

文化小叮嚀

Not all cultures share the same perspective on small talk and what constitutes a too-personal question. If you are not sure about social etiquette in a certain country, do some research, or talk to friends. During the first call, wait until you establish a business relationship before introducing small talk. Once you are familiar with the client, you may want to start calls with small talk.

並非所有的文化對於閒聊或是什麼構成太私人的問題持有同樣的看法。如果你不清楚某國的社交禮儀的話，可以先做一下調查，或是問問朋友。第一通電話中，與對方建立起商業關係之前，不要閒聊。一旦你和客戶變熟了，你就可以用閒話家常的方式來開啓每通電話。

Word List

perspective [pɚˋspɛktɪv] *n.* 看法；觀點
constitute [ˋkɑnstə͵tjut] *v.* 構成；組成
etiquette [ˋɛtɪkɛt] *n.* 禮儀；規矩
research [rɪˋsɝtʃ] *n./v.* 研究；調查
be familiar with sb./sth. 與某人熟稔；熟悉某事物
client [ˋklaɪənt] *n.* 顧客；委託人

4 實戰演練 Practice Exercises

I 請為下列三題選出最適本章的中文譯義。

1. small talk
   (A) 碎碎唸 (B) 八卦 (C) 閒聊
2. get down to business
   (A) 面對現實 (B) 開始上班 (C) 開始處理正事
3. bump up
   (A) 升等 (B) 撞上 (C) 提高

II 請根據你聽到的內容為下列兩題選出正確解答。

1. How is the economy in Taiwan?
   (A) Better than last year.
   (B) Not as good as last year.
   (C) The same as last year.
2. What did Daniel do last weekend?
   (A) He went hiking in the mountains.
   (B) He went skiing with his family.
   (C) He visited Taiwan for a 3-day weekend.

III 你和你要打電話聯絡的這位客戶關係還算不錯，談論正事前，你想稍微聊一下自己週末做了哪些事。利用下列詞語寫一篇短文模擬練習一下吧：

last weekend I did	to
have you ever been	show/exhibition/amusement park

＊解答請見 220 頁

轉入正題
Easing into Business

untitled

Send Now | Send Later | Save as Draft | Add Attachments | Signature | Options | Rewrap

To: Wallace Kuo

From: Peter Chen

Default Font | Text Size

Wallace:

Call Roland. We need the shipment details ASAP. I have to have them faxed to our manufacturer no later than tomorrow morning.

Thanks,
Peter

瓦勒斯：

打電話給洛藍。我們需要出貨細節，愈快愈好。我必須在明天早上以前將它們傳給我們的製造商。

謝謝，
彼得

1 Biz 必通句型 Need-to-Know Phrases

1.1 從閒聊切入正事
Moving from Small Talk to Business

❶ ..., I've got a/an ... to attend. Is there anything in particular you want to discuss?

……，我有一個……要參加。你有任何特別的事情想討論嗎？

例 Wallace, I've got a meeting to attend. Is there anything in particular you want to discuss?

瓦勒斯，我有一個會議要參加。你有任何特別的事情想討論嗎？

❷ ..., I know you're a busy person. I just wanted to discuss ...

……，我知道你是個大忙人。我只是想討論……。

例 Roland, I know you're a busy person. I just wanted to discuss some of my concerns regarding the colors you've chosen for the memory sticks.

洛藍，我知道你是個大忙人。我只是想討論幾個有關我對你為記憶卡所選的顏色的顧慮。

❸ ..., I know it's late in the day in (city/country), so ...

……，我知道現在（城市／國家）的時間很晚了，所以……。

例 Roland, I know it's late in the day in Berlin, so let me get right down to business.

洛藍，我知道現在柏林的時間很晚了，所以讓我立刻切入正題吧。

attend [ə`tɛnd] *v.* 出席；參加

particular [pə`tɪkjələ] *adj.* 特殊的；特定的（in particular 特別地）

concern [kən`sɝn] *n.* 關心的事；考量

❹ ..., I wanted to touch base with you ...

……，我想和你聯絡……。

例 Roland, I wanted to touch base with you on payment status.

洛藍，我想和你聯絡討論付款狀況。

❺ ..., I wanted to talk to you about ...

……，我想跟你談談關於……。

例 Roland, I wanted to talk to you about the first shipment of card readers.

洛藍，我想跟你談談關於讀卡機第一批貨的事。

❻ ..., I thought I should call and make sure everything is fine with ...

……，我覺得我應該打電話來確認……一切沒問題。

例 Roland, I thought I should call and make sure everything is fine with our last shipment.

洛藍，我覺得我應該打電話來確認我們上次出貨一切沒問題。

❼ ..., listen, I want to make sure we are on the same page with regard to ...

……，聽著，我想確認我們對於……的意見是一致的。

例 Roland, listen, I want to make sure we are on the same page with regard to memory stick colors.

洛藍，聽著，我想確認我們對於記憶卡顏色的意見是一致的。

❽ ..., I want to ask you ...

……，我想問你……。

例 Roland, I want to ask you a question regarding shipping.

洛藍，我想問你一個有關出貨的問題。

touch base *phr. v.* 聯絡
status [ˋstetəs] *n.* 狀態；情形；地位
shipment [ˋʃɪpmənt] *n.* 裝載的貨物；裝運
be on the same page 想法、意見一致

1.2 引入電談待議事項 Introducing the Call Agenda

❶ Let me give you my list of issues I think we need to discuss. First, ...
讓我告訴你我認為我們需要討論的幾個議題。首先，……。

例 Let me give you my list of issues I think we need to discuss. First, why don't we talk about shipping options?
讓我告訴你我認為我們需要討論的幾個議題。首先，我們何不談談關於出貨方式的選擇？

❷ ..., first let's discuss ...
……，首先我們來討論……。

例 Roland, first let's discuss the timeline for your order.
洛藍，首先我們來討論你的訂單的時間表。

❸ I think we should discuss ... first.
我認為我們應該先討論……。

例 I think we should discuss the payment terms first.
我認為我們應該先討論付款條件。

❹ A lot of these ... are interdependent. Let's deal with ... first.
這些……有很多是息息相關的。讓我們先處理……。

例 A lot of these product concerns are interdependent. Let's deal with color choices first.
這些產品的考量有很多是息息相關的。讓我們先處理顏色的選擇。

agenda [ə`dʒɛndə] *n.* 待議的各個事項；議程
option [`ɑpʃən] *n.* 選擇；可選擇的項目；選擇權
timeline [`taɪm͵laɪn] *n.* 時間表；時序表
terms [tɝmz] *n.*（複數形）（契約、談判等的）條件
interdependent [͵ɪntɚdɪ`pɛndənt] *adj.* 互相依賴的
deal with *phr. v.* 應付；處理；和……做生意

❺ There are a couple issues we need to talk about. Do you mind if we deal with ... first?

有幾個議題我們需要討論。你介不介意我們先處理……？

例 There are a couple issues we need to talk about. Do you mind if we deal with product <u>specs</u> first?

有幾個議題我們需要討論。你介不介意我們先處理產品規格？

❻ Second, I think we should talk about ...

其次，我認為我們應該討論……。

例 Second, I think we should talk about the method of delivery.

其次，我認為我們應該討論送貨方式。

❼ (Order), you have <u>a number of</u> options regarding ...

（順序），關於……你有幾個選擇。

例 Third, you have a number of options regarding <u>insurance</u>.

第三，關於保險你有幾個選擇。

❽ It would be great if we could <u>clear up</u> a couple of questions regarding ...

如果我們能釐清幾個有關……的問題就太好了。

例 It would be great if we could clear up a couple of questions I have regarding shipment dates.

如果我們能釐清我的幾個有關出貨日期的問題就太好了。

spec [spɛk] (=specification [ˌspɛsəfəˋkeʃən]) *n.*（常用複數）規格；詳細計劃書；說明書

a number of (things/people) 幾個（東西／人）

insurance [ɪnˋʃurəns] *n.* 保險

clear up *phr. v.* 整頓；清理；解決

2 實戰會話 Show Time

2.1 Dialogue

It's a busy day for Roland. He wants Wallace to get to the point.

Roland: So, what can I do for you, Wallace?

Wallace: Roland, I wanted to talk to you about shipping details.

Roland: Sure. What do you want to know?

Wallace: Listen, I want to make sure we are on the same page with regard to whether we are shipping FOB Origin or FOB Destination.

Roland: FOB Destination? What's that?

Wallace: Well, one of my American clients uses it. It means that we would be responsible for freight, other costs and risks. I assumed it was FOB Origin. I just wanted to touch base.

Roland: Ah, right. I've heard of that, too. But you assumed correctly. FOB Origin is what I understood.

Wallace: Great. Roland, I also wanted to ask you if you have any special shipping requests.

Roland: Yes, we need the stock ASAP.

對洛藍而言今天是忙碌的一天。他要瓦勒斯直接切入正題。

洛藍：　那麼，我能為你做什麼，瓦勒斯？

瓦勒斯：洛藍，我想跟你談談關於出貨的細節。

洛藍：　沒問題。你想知道什麼？

瓦勒斯：聽著，我想確認我們對要用 FOB 出貨點出貨還是 FOB 目的地出貨的意見是一致的。

洛藍：　FOB 目的地？那是什麼？

瓦勒斯：嗯，我的一個美國客戶用這種方式。它指的是我們將負擔運費、其他費用與風險。我想你應該是用 FOB 出貨點。我只是想聯絡一下。

洛藍：　啊，對。我也聽說過。不過你想得沒錯。我所瞭解的是 FOB 出貨點。

瓦勒斯：太好了。洛藍，我還想問你有沒有任何特別的運貨要求？

洛藍：　有，我們需要那筆貨，愈快愈好。

get to the point 談論重點 (= come to the point)
FOB Origin FOB 出貨點（Free On Board的縮寫，在此交易條件下，賣方承擔所有的風險，直到貨物裝載到指定的貨運公司或船舶上即履行交貨義務，其後貨物如在運輸途中有所損害，買方承擔所有損失，可向貨運公司進行索賠）
FOB Destination FOB 目的地（在此交易條件下，賣方承擔所有的風險，直到貨物運送到買方的碼頭後，風險才轉移給買方）
freight [fret] *n.* 運費；貨物；貨運
assume [ə`sjum] *v.* 假定；猜想；臆測
request [rɪ`kwɛst] *n./v.* 要求；請求
stock [stɑk] *n.* 進貨；存貨

2.2 Dialogue

Lucy has a number of issues she needs to discuss with Marie. She thinks they should talk about product colors first.

Marie: So what do we need to talk about, Lucy?

Lucy: Let me give you my list of issues I think we need to discuss. First, I think we should talk about your selection of product colors. Second, let's discuss the timeline for your order.

Marie: OK, let me <u>pull out</u> my notes. Right, I've got my notes.

Lucy: First, you have a number of options with regard to product specs. A lot of these product concerns are interdependent. Let's deal with color options first.

Marie: Well, all our products are a <u>combination</u> of <u>teal</u> blue, white and black.

Lucy: Right, that's what my notes say. But I also need you to confirm which is the <u>primary</u> color and the paint <u>finish</u>. You have a choice between <u>gloss</u>, <u>matte</u> and <u>flat</u>. So, you have three options for the <u>dominant</u> color and three options for finish.

Marie: That is a decision that Roland has to make. Maybe we can do better on your questions about the shipment dates.

譯文

露西有幾個議題需要和瑪莉討論。她認為她們應該先談產品顏色。

瑪莉：那我們需要談什麼呢，露西？

露西：讓我告訴妳我認為我們需要討論的幾個議題。首先，我覺得我們應該談談妳選擇的產品顏色。其次，我們來討論妳的訂單的時間表。

瑪莉：好，讓我拿一下我的筆記。好了，我拿到我的筆記了。

露西：首先，關於產品規格妳有幾個選擇。這些產品的考量有很多是息息相關的。讓我們先處理顏色的選擇。

瑪莉：嗯，我們所有的產品都是藍綠色、黑色和白色的組合。

露西：對，我的筆記上是這麼寫的。但我還需要妳確定哪一個是主色和漆面。妳可以選擇的有亮面、霧面和無上光。所以，主色妳有三種選擇，漆面也是三種選擇。

瑪莉：那是洛藍得做的決定。或許我們討論妳對出貨日期的問題會比較有結果。

Word List

pull out *phr. v.* 拉出；拿出
combination [ˌkɑmbə`neʃən] *n.* 混合；結合
teal [til] *adj./n.* 藍綠色（的）
primary [`praɪˌmɛrɪ] *adj.* 主要的；首要的
finish [`fɪnɪʃ] *n.* 面漆；表面作工
gloss [glɔs] *n.* 光澤；色澤
matte [mæt] *adj.* (= mat, matt) 無光澤的；褪光的
flat [flæt] *adj.*（色彩）無光澤的；均勻的；平坦的
dominant [`dɑmənənt] *adj.* 佔首位的；支配的

3 Biz 加分句型 Nice-to-Know Phrases

CD I-16

3.1 問題太多無法回答時 Too Many Questions to Answer

❶ **There are too many ... to discuss all at once. Can you prioritize them?**（希望客戶表明先後順序時）

一下子有太多的……要討論了。你可以排出它們的優先順序嗎？

例 There are too many product options to discuss all at once. Can you prioritize them?

一下子有太多的產品選擇要討論了。你可以排出它們的優先順序嗎？

❷ **That's a lot of options. Can you give me ... to think about this?**（需要一點時間思考時）

太多選擇了。你可以給我……想一下這個問題嗎？

例 That's a lot of options. Can you give me a few days to think about this?

太多選擇了。你可以給我幾天的時間想一下這個問題嗎？

❸ **Okay. I need to ... before I can discuss ...**（說明需要時間回覆的原因）

好。在我能討論……之前我需要……。

例 OK. I need to do some research before I can discuss changes to product specs.

好。在我能討論產品規格的變更之前我需要先作些調查。

❹ **Is it possible that you could fax me your list of ...?**（向客戶要求資料當作參考）

你有沒有可能可以把你（們）的……單傳真給我？

例 Is it possible that you could fax me your list of product changes?

你有沒有可能可以把你們的產品變動表傳真給我？

Word List

all at once 同時地；突然地

prioritize [praɪˋɔrəˌtaɪz] *v.* 排好……優先順序；給予……優先權

3.2 你不想做決定時 You Don't Want to Make a Decision

❶ I have to discuss ... with ...（不想或無法立即決定時）

我必須跟……討論……。

例 I have to discuss these changes with my manager.

我必須跟我的經理討論一下這些變動。

❷ I'll put that question on (person)'s desk and let him/her get back to you.（告訴客戶問題將由某人處理；當你無法、不想或疲於和這位客戶應對時）

我會把那個問題放在（某人）的桌上，由他／她來向您回覆。

例 I'll put that question on Sylvia's desk and let her get back to you.

我會把那個問題放在絲薇亞的桌上，由她來向您回覆。

❸ That would be a decision ... has/have to make.（當你無法決定時）

那是……得做的決定。

例 That would be a decision Kearny has to make.

那是柯尼得做的決定。

❹ I don't think it's possible, but let me see if I can talk ... into it.（用來婉拒及分擔責任）

我覺得不太可能，但是讓我看看我是不是能說服……同意。

例 I don't think it's possible, but let me see if I can talk my supervisor into it.

我覺得不太可能，但是讓我看看我是不是能說服我的上司同意。

talk sb. into N./Ving 說服某人做……

supervisor [ˏsupɚ`vaɪzɚ] *n.* 監督人；指導者；管理人；上司

小心陷阱

☹ 錯誤用法

There are **couple** issues we need to **talk to. The first,** can we deal with product specs?

有幾個議題我們需要討論。首先，我們能處理產品規格的問題嗎？

☺ 正確用法

There are **a couple of** issues we need to **talk about. First,** can we deal with product specs?

有幾個議題我們需要討論。首先，我們能處理產品規格的問題嗎？

文化小叮嚀

Canadians often perceive inexactness and vagueness as secretive. In fact, business people are encouraged by the Canadian government to urge their Asian business partners to communicate openly. Your openness about product quality, production processes and design will benefit your relationships with Canadians.

加拿大人通常視不精確和含糊其辭為有所隱瞞。事實上，加拿大政府鼓勵商務人士敦促他們的亞洲商業夥伴要坦然溝通。你對產品品質、製造過程與設計的坦然直率，將嘉惠你和加拿大人的關係。

perceive sb./sth. as sth. 認爲某人/某物是……

inexactness [ˌɪnɪgˋzæktnɪs] *n.* 不準確；不嚴密

vagueness [ˋvegnɪs] *n.* 含糊；曖昧

secretive [sɪˋkritɪv] *adj.* 隱密躲藏的

urge sb. to do sth. 力勸、敦促某人做某事

openness [ˋopənnɪs] *n.* 公開；率眞

 實戰演練 Practice Exercises

I 請為下列三題選出最適本章的中文譯義。

❶ touch base

(A) 達陣　(B) 上壘　(C) 聯絡

❷ on the same page

(A) 進度相同　(B) 溝通無礙　(C) 想法、意見一致

❸ get to the point

(A) 迅速完事　(B) 直敘重點　(C) 解釋清楚

II 請根據你聽到的內容為下列兩題選出正確解答。

CD I-17

❶ What does Jonathan want to decide on by the end of the week?

(A) The prices of the goods.

(B) The model numbers of the goods.

(C) The date the goods will be delivered.

❷ When will Terry email Jonathan?

(A) On Thursday afternoon.

(B) Before Thursday afternoon.

(C) Within a few minutes after they finish talking on the phone.

III 這次的案子進行地相當順利，你知道客戶有意購買產品，只需要一步步引導客戶討論就行了。打電話給客戶之前，利用下列詞語事先準備好說詞：

a couple	need to	talk about/discuss
first	do you mind	timeline/shipping

*解答請見 222 頁

聚集焦點
Gaining Focus

To: Sales Department

From: Peter Chen

Staff:

I know it is interesting to talk to people in foreign countries, but our phone bill is ridiculous. Let's keep our customers on track during your telephone discussions.

Peter
President
Omega Electronics, Taiwan

各位夥伴：

我知道和國外的人講話很有趣，但是我們的電話帳單太離譜了。請你們在用電話討論事情的時候，不要脫軌和客戶們聊些不相干的事。

彼得
台灣歐美嘉電子總裁

1 Biz 必通句型 Need-to-Know Phrases

CD I-18

1.1 減少選項 Narrowing Options

選擇太多未必是件好事，反而常讓人無法迅速做出決定。商談過程中可以先為客戶初步篩選，淘汰不可能及不適合的選項，以縮短客戶考慮的時間，讓溝通更順暢、工作更有效率。

❶ OK, (name). Let's try and narrow it down to just a few ...
好，（姓名）。我們試著把……縮減到只剩幾個。

例 OK, Sylvia. Let's try and narrow it down to just a few alternatives.
好，絲薇亞。我們試著把選擇縮減到只剩幾個。

❷ I think we need to reduce the number of ... first.
我認為我們應該先減少……的數目。

例 I think we need to reduce the number of sizes first.
我認為我們應該先減少尺寸的數目。

❸ (Name), let's see if we can get ... down to a manageable number.
（姓名），我們看看是不是能把……減到一個容易處理的數目。

例 Roland, let's see if we can get our color options down to a manageable number.
洛藍，我們看看是不是能把我們的色彩選擇減到一個容易處理的數目。

❹ Let's try and eliminate ... you are not interested in to save time.
我們試著刪除你沒有興趣的……以節省時間。

例 Let's try and eliminate the product features you are not interested in to save time.
我們試著刪除你沒有興趣的產品特性以節省時間。

Word List

narrow down sth. *phr. v.* 減少、縮小某事物
alternative [ɔlˋtɝnətɪv] *n.* 選擇；替換項目
reduce [rɪˋdjus] *v.* 減少；縮小；降低
manageable [ˋmænɪdʒəbl̩] *adj.* 易操縱的；可控制的
eliminate [ɪˋlɪmə͵net] *v.* 排除；消滅
feature [ˋfitʃɚ] *n.* 特徵；特色

❺ Let's discuss the relationship between ... and ... again.

我們再討論一次……和……之間的關係。

例 Let's discuss the relationship between product size and packaging again.

我們再討論一次產品尺寸和包裝之間的關係。

❻ I think that ... will have a considerable effect on ...

我想……對……的影響會很大。

例 I think that the sound card size will have a considerable effect on product packaging.

我想音效卡的尺寸對產品包裝的影響會很大。

❼ (Name), this decision is going to change ... with respect to ...

（姓名），這個決定將改變有關……的……。

例 Tina, this decision is going to change the possible size with respect to the logo.

蒂娜，這個決定將改變商標的可能尺寸。

❽ It's going to be difficult discussing ... and ... separately.

……和……分開討論會有困難。

例 It's going to be difficult discussing product color and color finish separately. Why don't we talk about them together?

產品顏色和顏色塗面分開討論會有困難。我們何不一併討論這兩項？

Word List

packaging [`pækɪdʒɪŋ] *n.* 包裝；包裝材料（如箱子、盒子等）

considerable [kən`sɪdərəbḷ] *adj.* 相當多的；相當大的

effect [ɪ`fɛkt] *n.* 影響；效果；作用

with respect to 關於

logo [`logo] *n.* 商標；標誌

separately [`sɛpərɪtlɪ] *adv.* 各別地；分離地

1.2 引領聽者回到議題 Bringing the Listener Back on Topic

談話時，很容易因爲討論其他相關事情而脫離原始主題；用下列八句將話題引回原始議題上。

1 (Name), can we get back to discussing ...?
(姓名)，我們能回過頭來討論……嗎？
例 Hans, can we get back to discussing my color options?
漢斯，我們能回過頭來討論我的顏色選擇嗎？

2 (Name), we need to agree on ... before we start discussing ...
(姓名)，開始討論……之前，我們需要對……取得共識。
例 Sylvia, we need to agree on lead time before we start discussing payment terms.
絲薇亞，開始討論付款條件之前，我們需要對前置時間取得共識。

3 I think we should return to our discussion of ... before we move on.
我覺得在往下進行之前，我們應該回到我們對……的討論。
例 I think we should return to our discussion of branding before we move on.
我覺得在往下進行之前，我們應該回到我們對品牌化的討論。

4 ... will impact our previous decision about ... Let's talk about ... again.
……將對我們先前有關……的決定產生影響。我們再談一次……。
例 Logo size will impact our previous decision about overall design. Let's talk about product specifications again.
商標尺寸將對我們先前有關整體設計的決定產生影響。我們再談一次產品規格。

Word List

get back to N./Ving 回到……
agree on sth. 一致同意某事
lead time [ˋlid ˏtaɪm] *n.* 前置作業期
move on *phr. v.* 前進；接著做……
branding [ˋbrændɪŋ] *n.* 品牌化（用設計、廣告等方式使消費者能辨識並記得某產品）
impact [ɪmˋpækt] *v.* 對……產生影響；衝擊
previous [ˋpriviəs] *adj.* 先前的
overall [ˋovɚˏɔl] *adj.* 全部的；整體的

❺ (Name), I still have a couple of questions regarding ... Can we revisit ...?

（姓名），關於……我仍舊有幾個疑問。我們能不能回頭討論……？

例 Tina, I still have a couple of questions regarding the draft. Can we revisit payment terms?

蒂娜，關於匯票我仍舊有幾個疑問。我們能不能回頭討論付款條件？

❻ (Name), do you mind if we return to our discussion of ...?

（姓名），你介不介意我們回到……的討論？

例 Timothy, do you mind if we return to our discussion of shipping dates?

提莫西，你介不介意我們回到出貨日期的討論？

❼ OK, let's go back and finish our discussion of ...

好，讓我們回頭完成我們……的討論。

例 OK, let's go back and finish our discussion of the budget for advertising.

好，讓我們回頭完成我們對廣告預算的討論。

❽ Can we get back to our agenda, (name)?

我們能不能回到我們的議程，（姓名）？

例 Can we get back to our agenda, Hans?

我們能不能回到我們的議程，漢斯？

revisit [ri`vɪzɪt] *v.* 重臨；再訪

draft [dræft] *n.* 匯票；草稿

budget [`bʌʤɪt] *n./v.* 預算；經費

advertising [`ædvɚˌtaɪzɪŋ] *n.* 做廣告；廣告

2 實戰會話 Show Time

2.1 Dialogue

Wallace and Roland start sorting out the details regarding product color, logo size, etc. Their first goal, however, is to decide which to discuss first.

Wallace: OK, Roland. Let's try and narrow it down to just a few colors.

Roland: I agree. I think we need to reduce the number of color options first.

Wallace: OK. First, do you want the card readers and memory sticks the same color or do you want their colors to complement each other?

Roland: Well, our policy is to have all our products the same color. But I like the idea of complementary colors. We might be able to access a new demographic.

Wallace: OK. Sounds great. Let's discuss the relationship between the logo and product specifications again.

Roland: Well ... the logo has to be large enough to be identifiable.

Wallace: Right. But I think that the logo size will have a considerable effect on product packaging, if the product design has to be changed.

譯文

瓦勒斯和洛藍開始整理有關產品顏色、商標尺寸等細節。然而，他們的首要目標是決定應該先討論什麼。

瓦勒斯：好，洛藍。我們試著把顏色縮減到只剩幾個吧。

洛藍：　我同意。我認為我們應該先減少色彩選擇的數目。

瓦勒斯：好。首先，你希望讀卡機和記憶卡是同樣顏色還是你希望用不同的顏色互搭？

洛藍：　這個嘛，我們的政策是所有的產品都使用相同顏色。但是我喜歡顏色互搭這個主意。我們也許能接近新客群。

瓦勒斯：好，聽起來很棒。我們再討論一次商標和產品規格之間的關係。

洛藍：　呃……商標要大到能清楚辨識才行。

瓦勒斯：好。不過我想商標尺寸對產品包裝的影響會很大，如果產品設計必須被改變的話。

Word List

sort out *phr. v.* 整理；分類；釐清；解決
complement [`kɑmplə͵mɛnt] *v.* 補足；與……相配
policy [`pɑləsɪ] *n.* 政策；方針
complementary [͵kɑmplə`mɛntərɪ] *adj.* 互補的；相配的
access [`æksɛs] *v.* 接近；可取得……的管道（access to sth. 使用、獲得某事物的管道）
demographic [͵dɛmə`græfɪk] *n.* 顧客群
identifiable [aɪ`dɛntə͵faɪəbl̩] *adj.* 能辨識的；可識別的

2.2 Dialogue

Lucy and Marie have a similar conversation and, interestingly, encounter a similar problem.

Marie: Lucy, can we get back to discussing the color options?

Lucy: Sure, let's see if we can get the options down to a manageable number.

Marie: Right. Well, I know we were looking at the colors in the blue-green range.

Lucy: OK, my notes say you also have three paint finishes to choose from: matte, gloss, and high gloss.

Marie: OK, let's start with the finishes. But Lucy, I think we should return to our discussion of branding before we move on.

Lucy: Why do you say that?

Marie: This decision about logo size is going to change the possibilities with respect to overall color choice.

Lucy: Exactly. We should return to our discussion about branding.

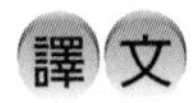

露西和瑪莉有一段類似的對話，而且有趣的是，也遇到一個類似的問題。

瑪莉：露西，我們能回過頭來討論顏色的選擇嗎？

露西：當然，我們看看是不是能把選項減到一個容易處理的數目。

瑪莉：對。呃，我知道我們在考慮藍綠色系的顏色。

露西：好，我的筆記說你們也有三種漆面可選擇：霧面、亮面和超亮面。

瑪莉：好，我們從漆面開始吧。不過露西，我覺得在往下進行之前，我們應該回到我們對品牌化的討論。

露西：妳為什麼這麼說？

瑪莉：這個關於商標尺寸的決定將改變整體顏色選擇的可能。

露西：一點也沒錯。我們應該回到對品牌化的討論。

Word List

encounter [ɪn`kaʊntɚ] *v.* 遭遇；遇見
range [rendʒ] *n.* 範圍；區域
possibility [ˌpɑsə`bɪlətɪ] *n.* 可能性；可能的事
exactly [ɪg`zæktlɪ] *adv.*（用於回答應和）一點也沒錯；確切地

3 加分句型 Nice-to-Know Phrases

CD I-20

3.1 當你的客戶不同意但你是對的時 When Your Client Disagrees but You Are Right

❶ **I disagree. We have to discuss ... first.**（應該堅持時）

我不同意。我們必須先討論……。

例 I disagree. We have to discuss logo size first.

我不同意。我們必須先討論商標尺寸。

❷ **I think it would be better if we discuss ... first.**（語氣婉轉）

我想先討論……的話會比較好。

例 I think it would be better if we discuss logo size first.

我想先討論商標尺寸的話會比較好。

❸ **I've been through this issue of ... a number of times.**（讓客戶知道你有一定的經驗）

我已經處理過好幾次這種……的問題。

例 I've been through this issue of logo size a number of times. This is the easy way.

我已經處理過好幾次這種商標尺寸的問題。這是簡單的方式。

❹ **I'm sorry, (name). This is the best way to sort this out.**（表示沒有更好的方法了）

對不起，（姓名）。這是解決這個問題最好的辦法。

例 I'm sorry, David. This is the best way to sort this out.

對不起，大衛。這是解決這個問題最好的辦法。

Word List

disagree [ˌdɪsəˋgri] *v.* 不贊同；不一致

sb. has been through sth. 某人曾經歷、遭遇過某事

3.2 當你的客戶抗拒時 When Your Client Resists

❶ We have to get back to our discussion of ...（說服客戶重新討論）

我們必須回到我們對……的討論。

例 We have to get back to our discussion of logo size.

我們必須回到我們對商標尺寸的討論。

❷ If we discuss ... first, we'll ...（告訴客戶可能的結果）

如果我們先討論……的話，我們會……。

例 If we discuss product color first, we'll come to the wrong decision.

如果我們先討論產品顏色的話，我們會做出錯誤的決定。

❸ You'll have to trust me. We need to discuss ... first.（爭取客戶的信任）

你必須相信我。我們需要先討論……。

例 You'll have to trust me. We need to discuss logo size first.

你必須相信我。我們需要先討論商標尺寸。

❹ (Name), trust me on this one. I know I'm right.（表示絕對的信心）

（姓名），這件事情就相信我。我知道我是對的。

例 Tania, trust me on this one. I know I'm right.

坦妮雅，這件事情就相信我。我知道我是對的。

resist [rɪ`zɪst] *v.* 反抗；抵抗

come to sth. 達成……；演變成……

小心陷阱

☹ 錯誤用法

Discuss product color and finish **separate are** difficult. Why don't we talk about them **togather**?

很難將產品顏色和漆面分開來討論。我們何不一併討論？

☺ 正確用法

Discussing product color and finish **separately is** difficult. Why don't we talk about them **together**?

很難將產品顏色和漆面分開來討論。我們何不一併討論？

文化小叮嚀

Japanese business people sometimes consider oral agreements binding and don't always create detailed contracts that account for all possible problems. Maintaining a good record of discussions during telephone negotiations will reduce misunderstanding and provide you with a valuable written record.

日本的商人有時認為口頭上的同意具有約束力，不一定會制訂詳細的合約對應所有可能發生的問題。保存電話協商時完整的討論記錄將能減少誤會，也可以提供你一份有用的書面記錄。

oral [`orəl] *adj.* 口述的；口部的

binding [`baɪndɪŋ] *adj.* 有約束力的；必須遵守的

account for (sth.) 對某事作解釋；對某事負責

maintain [men`ten] *v.* 維持；保養

provide sb. with sth. 提供某人某事物

4 實戰演練 Practice Exercises

I 請為下列三題選出最適本章的中文譯義。

1. narrow something down to ...

   (A) 放棄某事物改採…… (B) 將某事物縮減為…… (C) 確定某事物為……

2. with respect to ...

   (A) 向……致敬 (B) 關於…… (C) 連同……

3. get back to ...

   (A) 回電給…… (B) 還給…… (C) 回到……

II 請根據你聽到的內容為下列三題選出正確解答。

CD I-21

1. What was the original agreed method of payment?

   (A) CAD.

   (B) COD.

   (C) Cash in advance.

2. Who made the decision to change the payment terms?

   (A) The production manager.

   (B) The financial manager.

   (C) The purchasing manager.

3. When will Sylvia probably call Greta back?

   (A) Tomorrow evening.

   (B) Tomorrow afternoon.

   (C) Tomorrow morning.

III 由於你是最了解產品特色的人，因此妥善地引導對話使商談節奏更流暢非常重要。打電話給客戶之前，利用下列詞語寫一篇短文模擬一下實境吧。

are interrelated	return to	impact
discuss	access	eliminate

＊解答請見 224 頁

總結重點
Summarizing Key Points

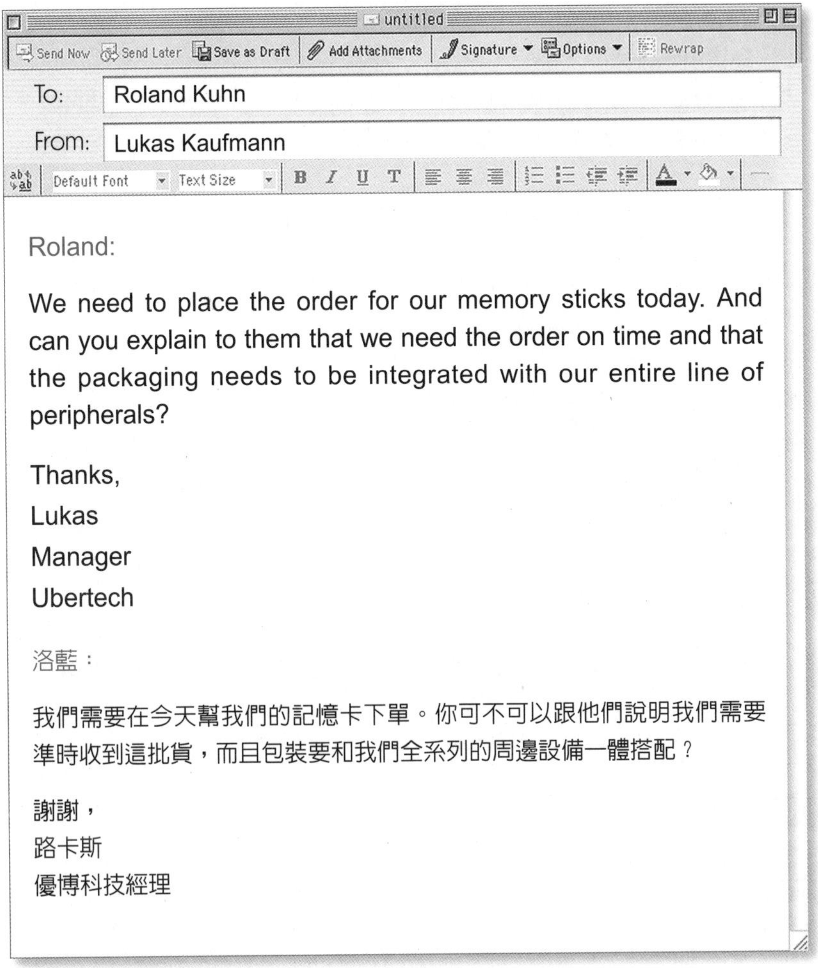

untitled

Send Now | Send Later | Save as Draft | Add Attachments | Signature | Options | Rewrap

To: Roland Kuhn

From: Lukas Kaufmann

Default Font | Text Size

Roland:

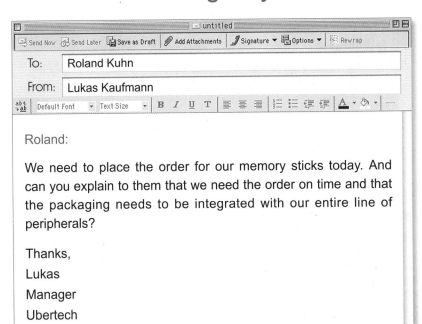

We need to place the order for our memory sticks today. And can you explain to them that we need the order on time and that the packaging needs to be integrated with our entire line of peripherals?

Thanks,
Lukas
Manager
Ubertech

洛藍：

我們需要在今天幫我們的記憶卡下單。你可不可以跟他們說明我們需要準時收到這批貨，而且包裝要和我們全系列的周邊設備一體搭配？

謝謝，
路卡斯
優博科技經理

1 Biz 必通句型 Need-to-Know Phrases

CD I-22

1.1 導入重點 Introducing Key Points

下列八句用來告訴對方你關切的第一事項。

❶ The main focus should be on ...

主要重點應該放在……。

例 The main focus should be on getting us the product on time.

主要重點應該放在準時把產品交給我們。

❷ Our major concern is ...

我們的主要考量是……。

例 Our major concern is just-in-time delivery.

我們的主要考量是及時運送。

❸ The most important factor is ...

最重要的因素是……。

例 The most important factor is the packaging design.

最重要的因素是包裝設計。

❹ Our No. 1 issue is ...

我們的首要議題是……。

例 Our No. 1 issue is that the packaging works with the rest of our products.

我們的首要議題是包裝要和我們其餘的產品搭配。

Word List

focus [`fokəs] *n.* 焦點；重點／*v.* 聚焦 (+ on sth.)

on time 準時

just-in-time [`ʤʌstɪn,taɪm] *adj.* 及時的（Just-In-Time Delivery 及時運送，指不過早亦不延遲，於需要的時間運送）

factor [`fæktɚ] *n.* 因素；要素

❺ Our focus is on ...

我們把重點放在……。

例 Our focus is on offering reliable products to our customers at the lowest possible price.

我們把重點放在以可能的最低價格將可靠的產品提供給我們的客戶。

❻ What we are looking for is ...

我們正在尋找的是……。

例 What we are looking for is a product that will get customers through the door.

我們正在尋找的是一個能讓顧客上門的產品。

❼ Our primary goal is ...

我們的首要目標是……。

例 Our primary goal is to shorten the turnaround time between the order and receiving the product.

我們的首要目標是縮短自下單到收到產品的這一段時間。

❽ We need some assurance that …

我們需要一些保證確定……。

例 We need some assurance that the product will arrive on time.

我們需要一些保證確定產品會準時抵達。

Word List

reliable [rɪ`laɪəbḷ] *adj.* 可靠的；可信賴的

get customers through the door 吸引顧客上門

primary [`praɪ͵mɛrɪ] *adj.* 首要的；基本的

shorten [`ʃɔrtn̩] *v.* 減少；縮短

turnaround [`tɝnə͵raʊnd] *n.*（工作）自接下至完成送回的時間；往返時間

assurance [ə`ʃʊrəns] *n.* 保證；自信

1.2 開啓討論 Opening a Discussion

打開話匣的方式有很多種，下列三句以詢問的方式。

❶ Do you have any ideas regarding ...?

關於……，你有沒有什麼想法？

例 Do you have any ideas regarding a different packaging design?

關於不同的包裝設計，你有沒有什麼想法？

❷ What ... do you need?

你需要什麼……？

例 What kind of assurance do you need?

你需要什麼樣的保證？

❸ Can you expand on ...?

你能不能進一步說明……？

例 Can you expand on your ideas about advertising and brand image further?

你能不能更進一步說明你對廣告與品牌形象的看法？

下列五句採直述的方式。

❹ I wouldn't mind if we talked about ... a bit more.

我不介意我們再多談一點……。

例 I wouldn't mind if we talked about price a bit more.

我不介意我們再多談一點價格方面的事。

Word List

expand on/upon (sth.) 詳述（某事物）

advertising [`ædvɚ͵taɪzɪŋ] *n.* 廣告（業）；做廣告

brand image [`brænd ͵ɪmɪʤ] *n.* 品牌形象（消費者對品牌持有的感覺與印象）

a bit more 多一點（反義爲 a bit less 少一點）

❺ Let's talk some more about ...

我們再多談一點⋯⋯。

例 Let's talk some more about how we can develop this product line.

我們再多談一點我們該如何開發這系列的產品。

❻ I need you to clarify your position on ...

我需要你闡明你對⋯⋯的立場。

例 I need you to clarify your position on merchandise planning for this season.

我需要你闡明你對這季商品規畫的立場。

❼ You mentioned ... I need some more information about ...

你提過⋯⋯。我需要更多有關⋯⋯的資料。

例 You mentioned that the product packaging was unacceptable. I need some more detailed information about the problem with the packaging.

你提過這項產品包裝難以接受。我需要更多有關包裝問題的詳細資料。

❽ I'd like to discuss this issue of ...

我想討論這個⋯⋯的議題。

例 I'd like to discuss this issue of improving customer satisfaction ratings.

我想討論這個改善顧客滿意度的議題。

Word List

product line [`prɑdəkt ˏlaɪn] *n.* 產品線；產品系列

position [pə`zɪʃən] *n.* 立場；態度 (+ on sth.)

merchandise planning [`mɝtʃənˏdaɪz ˏplænɪŋ] *n.* 商品規劃

unacceptable [ˏʌnək`sɛptəbl̩] *adj.* 不能接受的；難以認可的

satisfaction [ˏsætɪs`fækʃən] *n.* 滿意；滿足

ratings [`retɪŋz] *n.*（複數形）評分；評比

2 實戰會話 Show Time

CD I-23

2.1 Dialogue

Roland is explaining his principal concerns about the memory sticks to Wallace.

Roland: The main focus should be on getting us the product on time.

Wallace: I understand. We'll do our best to make sure that the shipment arrives as scheduled.

Roland: Wallace, we will need some assurance that the product will arrive on time.

Wallace: That shouldn't be a problem. Do you have any concerns about the product?

Roland: Well, we weren't very happy with the packaging. It wasn't what we expected.

Wallace: What was wrong with the packaging?

Roland: The colors were correct, but the design didn't fit with the rest of our products. The most important factor is packaging design. It needs to belong to our product family. Our No. 1 issue is that the packaging fits with the rest of our products.

譯文

洛藍正在對瓦勒斯說明他對記憶卡的主要顧慮。

洛藍：　主要重點應該放在準時把產品交給我們。

瓦勒斯：我瞭解。我們會盡全力確定貨物如預定時間抵達。

洛藍：　瓦勒斯，我們需要一些保證確定產品會準時抵達。

瓦勒斯：那應該不是問題。關於產品你們有沒有什麼考量？

洛藍：　呃，我們對包裝不是很滿意。它不是我們所預期的。

瓦勒斯：包裝哪裡不對？

洛藍：　顏色對了，但設計和我們其餘產品並不搭。最重要的因素是包裝設計，它需要跟我們的產品系列一體。我們的首要議題是包裝能和我們其餘的產品搭配。

Word List

principal [`prɪnsəpḷ] *adj.* 主要的；首要的
schedule [`skɛdʒʊl] *v.* 安排；預定／*n.* 時間表；計劃表
fit with (sth.) 和（某事物）搭配
belong to ... 屬於……
product family [`prɑdəkt ˏfæməlɪ] *n.* 產品系列

2.2 Dialogue

Lucy and Marie are discussing the turnaround between when an order is placed and when Ubertech receives it.

Lucy: Do you have any ideas regarding the delay between when an order is placed and when it is received?

Marie: Sure. Right now the needs of consumers are changing very quickly. We'd like to be able to meet these needs as soon as we identify them.

Lucy: Can you expand on faster turnaround?

Marie: Well, what I mean is that consumers are gravitating toward certain product configurations. And this happens very quickly. We want to be able to offer that product as quickly as possible. That means we need the products fast.

Lucy: Mmm ... I understand. Is there any product in particular you're talking about?

Marie: Memory sticks. Our competition is beating us. They are introducing larger capacity sticks every week. We need to receive smaller shipments and have them on the shelves in a week or less.

Lucy: I see.

露西和瑪莉正在討論自下單之後到優博科技收到貨物所需的時間。

露西：關於訂單自下單到收貨間時間上的延誤，妳有沒有什麼想法？

瑪莉：當然有。現在顧客的需求變得非常快。我們希望一旦發現有需求就能加以滿足。

露西：妳能不能進一步說明妳所謂的更快的完交時間？

瑪莉：呃，我的意思是顧客會受到某種產品結構吸引，而且這發生得非常快。我們想要能夠盡快提供那樣產品。這表示我們需要快速得到產品。

露西：嗯……我瞭解了。妳有特定在指哪一項產品嗎？

瑪莉：記憶卡。我們的競爭對手正在超越我們。他們每週推出更大容量的記憶卡。我們需要接收較少量的貨，並在一個星期或更短的時間之內將它們上架。

露西：我知道了。

Word List

delay [dɪ`le] *n./v.* 延誤；耽擱
meet someone's needs 滿足某人的需求
identify [aɪ`dɛntə,faɪ] *v.* 識別；發現；確定
gravitate [`grævə,tet] *v.* 被吸引（gravitate toward/to sth./sb. 受某事物／某人吸引）
configuration [kən,fɪgjə`reʃən] *n.* 結構；表面配置
in particular 特別地
competition [,kɑmpə`tɪʃən] *n.* 競爭對手；競爭；比賽
beat [bit] *v.* 超越；打敗；打；擊
capacity [kə`pæsətɪ] *n.* 容量；容積；能力

3 Biz 加分句型 Nice-to-Know Phrases

CD I-24

3.1 客戶的態度不確定 The Client Is Not Being Definitive

當你抓不到客戶的談話重點時，可用下列四句請對方說清楚、講明白。

❶ **I need you to narrow down ...**（請對方縮小話題範圍）

我需要你再說仔細一點……。

例 I need you to narrow down your concerns about product price.

我需要你再說仔細一點你對產品價格的考量。

❷ **What I need is a clear understanding of ...**（告訴對方你想知道的事）

我需要的是清楚瞭解……。

例 What I need is a clear understanding of your problems with the product.

我需要的是清楚瞭解你對產品的疑問。

❸ **I need you to tell me exactly what ...**（要求對方具體說明）

我需要你清楚地告訴我……是什麼。

例 I need you to tell me exactly what your concern is.

我需要你清楚地告訴我你的顧慮是什麼。

❹ **I don't understand. What exactly is ...?**（直接提出疑問）

我不懂。……到底是什麼？

例 I don't understand. What exactly is the problem with the prototype?

我不懂。原樣的問題到底出在哪裡？

definitive [dɪˋfɪnətɪv] *adj.* 可靠的；確定的

prototype [ˋprotəˏtaɪp] *n.*（量產前的）原型；模範

3.2 你的客戶不懂你的意思 Your Customer Isn't Getting Your Message

溝通最大的難處在於雙方是否能夠彼此理解；當你察覺對方不是很懂你要表達的意思時，可用下列四句再說明一次（四句談論同樣的主題，以彰顯語氣的差異）。

❶ What I mean is ...（重述立場）

我的意思是……。

例 What I mean is that this product is not what we are looking for.

我的意思是這個產品不是我們要找的。

❷ I am saying ...（直接表明）

我說的是……。

例 I am saying that this product is not what we are looking for.

我說的是這個產品不是我們要找的。

❸ I am trying to say ...（再次解說）

我想說的是……。

例 I am trying to say that this product is not what we are looking for.

我想說的是這個產品不是我們要找的。

❹ Let me rephrase that. ...（改變說法）

讓我換個方式說吧。……。

例 Let me rephrase that. This product is not what we are looking for.

讓我換個方式說吧。這個產品不是我們要找的。

Word List

rephrase [ri`frez] *v.* 改變措詞表達

小心陷阱

☹ 錯誤用法

Colors were correct, but **design** didn't **fit to rest** of our products.

顏色是正確的，但設計和我們其餘的產品不搭。

☺ 正確用法

The colors were correct, but **the design** didn't **fit with the rest** of our products.

顏色是正確的，但設計和我們其餘的產品不搭。

文化小叮嚀

When you are in the Philippines, you need to take extra care with your appearance. Filipinos consider how you dress to be a reflection of not only your professionalism, but also your social status. Dress conservatively until you are certain of how formal or informal your attire should be.

當你在菲律賓時，你得特別注意你的外表。菲律賓人認為你的穿著方式不只反映你的專業，也反映你的社會地位。穿著保守一點，直到你很確定你的衣著該如何正式或非正式為止。

Word List

the Philippines [ðə `fɪlə,pinz] *n.* 菲律賓（由七千多個島嶼組成）

appearance [ə`pɪrəns] *n.* 外表；顯露

Filipino [,fɪlə`pino] *n.* 菲律賓人／*adj.* 菲律賓（人）的

reflection [rɪ`flɛkʃən] *n.* 反映；反射

professionalism [prə`fɛʃənḷ,ɪzəm] *n.* 專門技術；專家氣質

social status [`soʃəl ,stetəs] *n.* 社會地位

conservatively [kən`sɝvətɪvlɪ] *adv.* 保守地

attire [ə`taɪr] *n.*（不可數）衣著；服裝

4 實戰演練 Practice Exercises

I 請為下列三題選出最適本章的中文譯義。

❶ on time

(A) 及時 (B) 準時 (C) 定時

❷ fit with ...

(A) 和……處得來 (B) 與……相搭 (C) 跟……一樣

❸ gravitate toward ...

(A) 被…… 影響 (B) 遭……控制 (C) 受……吸引

II 請根據你聽到的內容為下列兩題選出正確解答。

❶ What does the man want to do?

(A) Make major changes to the product.

(B) Make minor changes to the product specs.

(C) Market the product in a different way.

❷ What does the woman think needs to be changed about the product?

(A) Its specs.

(B) Its design.

(C) Its price.

III 你需要打電話給供應商要求他們準時交貨，並順道「提醒」一下遲交可能造成的後果。拿起話筒之前，利用下列詞語寫一篇短文模擬演練一下吧。

what I am saying	we need some assurance
some more about	lose money
even more importantly	get the shipment on time

＊解答請見 226 頁

結束通話
Ending a Call

untitled

Send Now | Send Later | Save as Draft | Add Attachments | Signature | Options | Rewrap

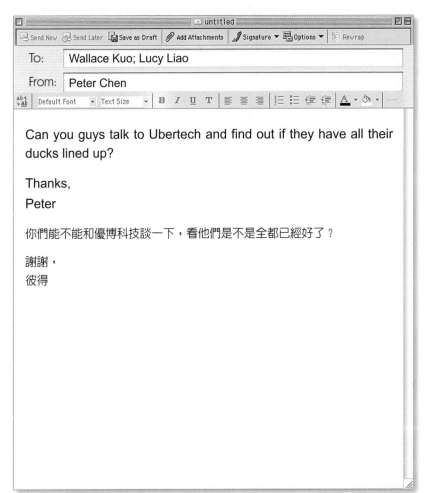

To: Wallace Kuo; Lucy Liao

From: Peter Chen

Default Font | Text Size

Can you guys talk to Ubertech and find out if they have all their ducks lined up?

Thanks,
Peter

你們能不能和優博科技談一下，看他們是不是全都已經好了？

謝謝，
彼得

1 Biz 必通句型 Need-to-Know Phrases

CD I-26

1.1 快速結束 A Quick Conclusion

用下列四句詢問對方是否還需要其他協助，將談話引至末端準備結束。

❶ **(Name), is there anything else I can help you with?**
（姓名），還有其他事我能幫你的嗎？

例 Tania, is there anything else I can help you with?
坦妮雅，還有其他事我能幫妳的嗎？

❷ **Do you have any other ... concerns?**
你還有任何其他……的顧慮嗎？

例 Do you have any other product concerns?
你還有任何其他產品的顧慮嗎？

❸ **Can I provide you with any other information regarding ...?**
關於……，我還能提供你任何其他的資訊嗎？

例 Can I provide you with any other information regarding our new models?
關於我們的新型號，我還能提供你任何其他的資訊嗎？

❹ **Are there any other issues you want to discuss regarding ...?**
關於……，你還有任何其他問題想討論的嗎？

例 Are there any other issues you want to discuss regarding this order?
關於這份訂單，你還有任何其他問題想討論的嗎？

Word List

conclusion [kən`kluʒən] *n.* 結束；結論
provide sb. with sth. 提供某人某事物
model [`mɑdl̩] *n.* 型號；樣式；模型

下列三句爲結束談話時常用的禮貌說辭。

❺ I hope I've been of some assistance, (name).

我希望我所做的有所幫助，（姓名）。

例 I hope I've been of some assistance, Mr. Chou.

我希望我所做的有所幫助，周先生。

❻ It's been good to hear from you. I'm glad we reached an agreement on ...

能接到你的電話真好。很高興我們就……達成了協議。

例 It's been good to hear from you. I'm glad we reached an agreement on contract requirements.

能接到你的電話真好。很高興我們就合約規定達成了協議。

❼ Well, that just about covers it. Call me if you have any problems with ...

嗯，這樣差不多都涵蓋到了。如果你對……有任何問題就打電話給我。

例 Well, that just about covers it, Gretchen. Call me if you have any problems with the shipment.

嗯，這樣差不多都涵蓋到了，葛瑞倩。如果妳對運貨有任何問題就打電話給我。

最後這句用來答謝對方的協助，並將對話正式結束。

❽ Thanks for your help. I'll ring you again if I need more information regarding ...

謝謝你的幫忙。如果我需要更多有關……的資料，我會再打電話給你。

例 Thanks for your help, Hans. I'll ring you again if I need more information regarding the quote.

謝謝你的幫忙，漢斯。如果我需要更多有關報價的資料，我會再打電話給你。

hear from sb. 接到某人的電話或信件

reach an agreement on sth. 就某事達成協議

requirement [rɪ`kwaɪrmənt] *n.* 規定；條件；需要

cover [`kʌvɚ] *v.* 包含；覆蓋

ring [rɪŋ] *v.* 打電話；（鈴）響

quote [kwot] *n.* 報價

1.2 結束通話 Getting Off the Phone

如果談話的時間或內容超過你的預期時，可用下列八句委婉請退。

❶ Listen, (name), I have...

聽著，（姓名），我有……。

例 Listen, David, I have a meeting in five minutes I have to attend.

聽著，大衛，五分鐘後我有一個會議必須參加。

❷ I'm sorry, but I forgot to mention that I have ...

對不起，我忘記說我有……。

例 I'm sorry, Roland, but I forgot to mention that I have a meeting in 10 minutes.

對不起，洛藍，我忘記說 10 分鐘後我有一個會議。

❸ I'm sorry, but I have to run. I have ...

對不起，但我必須走了。我有……。

例 I'm sorry, but I have to run. I have a meeting waiting for me.

對不起，但我必須走了。我有個會議在等我。

❹ I have to get going. Can I call you back ...?

我必須走了。我可以……再打電話給你嗎？

例 I have to get going. Can I call you back tomorrow?

我必須走了。我可以明天再打電話給你嗎？

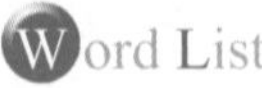

get off *phr. v.* 離開
forget to do sth. 忘記做某事（forget doing sth. 忘了做過某件事）
mention [`mɛnʃən] *v.* 提到；說起
have to run 必須離開
have to get going 必須要走了

❺ Can we discuss this later, when ...?

我們能不能晚一點再討論這個，在……的時候？

例 Can we discuss this later, when I get back to the office?

我們能不能晚一點再討論這個，在我回到辦公室的時候？

❻ Would you mind if we talk about this again later? I have ...

你介意我們晚點再來談這個嗎？我有……。

例 Would you mind if we talk about this again later? I have an important meeting I have to attend.

你介意我們晚點再來談這個嗎？我有個重要的會議必須出席。

❼ Will you have time (when) to continue this discussion? I have to ...

（某時）你會有時間繼續這項討論嗎？我必須……。

例 Will you have time on Tuesday to continue this discussion? I have to talk to our supplier first.

星期二你會有時間繼續這項討論嗎？我必須先和我們的供應商談一下。

❽ I can't talk right now. I have ...

我現在不能談。我有……。

例 I can't talk right now. I have a doctor's appointment in one hour.

我現在不能談。一小時後我有預約門診要看醫生。

supplier [səˋplaɪɚ] *n.* 供應商

appointment [əˋpɔɪntmənt] *n.*（會面的）約定；（正式的）約會

2 實戰會話 Show Time

2.1 Dialogue

Lucy wants to double-check that Marie is OK with the shipment dates.

Lucy: Marie, I'm just calling to make sure everything is fine on your end.

Marie: No problem, everything is great.

Lucy: Are there any issues you want to discuss regarding the shipping date?

Marie: No, I think we've covered all the bases.

Lucy: Great! I just wanted to check that we've covered all the bases. Developing a new working relationship always seems to involve a lot of discussion. I'm glad we reached an agreement on the shipment dates.

Marie: Me, too. Let me tell you, this hasn't been half as bad as when we ordered laptop cases from a company in Russia. I'm glad you called. It's been good to hear from you.

Lucy: Well, that just about covers it. Call me if you have any problems.

譯文

露西想再次確定瑪莉覺得裝運日期沒問題。

露西：瑪莉，我打來只是想確定妳那邊一切都很好。

瑪莉：沒問題，一切都很順利。

露西：關於出貨日期，妳還有任何問題想討論的嗎？

瑪莉：沒有，我想重要的項目我們已經全都說到了。

露西：很好！我只是想確定我們涵蓋了所有重要的項目。建立一段新的合作關係似乎總是需要經過許多討論。很高興我們就裝運日期達成了協議。

瑪莉：我也是。我告訴妳，這還沒有我們向俄羅斯一家公司訂購手提電腦包一半的麻煩呢。很高興妳打來，能接到妳的電話真好。

露西：呃，這樣差不多（都涵蓋到）了。如果妳有任何問題就打電話給我。

Word List

double-check [`dʌbḷ`tʃɛk] *v.* 複查
on your end 你那邊；你那端
cover all the bases 涵蓋所有重要的部分
involve [ɪn`vɑlv] *v.* 需要；包含；牽涉
half as bad as ... 如……一半的糟
laptop [`læp,tɑp] *n.* 膝上型電腦；筆記型電腦

2.2 Dialogue

Wallace talks to Roland to ensure he is happy with final product design.

Wallace: Roland, I just wanted to give you a call to see if you are still happy with the design.

Roland: Hi, Wallace. Sure things are fine. I ran it past the team one more time and there weren't any complaints or questions.

Wallace: I'm happy to hear that. I also wanted to talk to you about a new product we'll be introducing next week.

Roland: I'm sorry, but I've got to run. I have a meeting in 10 minutes.

Wallace: I understand. Would you mind if we talked about this again later? Can I call you back tomorrow?

Roland: Sure, no problem. Listen, Wallace, I have a meeting in the morning I have to attend, but I'll be free in the afternoon.

Wallace: OK. That sounds great. I'll talk to you then.

譯文

瓦勒斯和洛藍講話以確定他對最後的產品設計感到滿意。

瓦勒斯：洛藍，我只是想打電話過來，看你是不是還滿意這個設計。

洛藍： 嗨，瓦勒斯。當然一切都很好。我又讓團隊看了一次，並沒有任何的抱怨或疑問。

瓦勒斯：很高興聽到你這麼說。我還想跟你聊一下我們下個禮拜即將推出的一個新產品。

洛藍： 對不起，但我必須走了。 10 分鐘後我有個會議。

瓦勒斯：我瞭解。你介意我們晚點再來談這個嗎？我可以明天再打電話給你嗎？

洛藍： 當然，沒問題。聽著，瓦勒斯，我早上有一個會議要出席，但下午會有空。

瓦勒斯：好，聽起來很好。到時候我再跟你聊。

Word List

ensure [ɪn`ʃʊr] *v.* 確保；保證；擔保
run sth. past someone 向某人提及某事；告知某人某事（以看他們對此事的反應或意見）
complaint [kəm`plent] *n.* 抱怨；抗議

3 Biz 加分句型 Nice-to-Know Phrases

CD I-28

3.1 你需要中斷一下 You Need a Minute

除了插播之外（見第十章加分句型 3.1），講電話經常會因爲外在因素干擾而稍微中斷；如果你很快就能排除這些因素繼續通話的話，可用下列四句請對方稍等一下。

❶ **Could you please <u>hold on</u> for ..., so that I can ...?**（當你需要拿參考資料等稍微離開一下時）
能不能請你稍等……，好讓我能……？

例 Could you please hold on for a second, so that I can get the file, Timothy?
提莫西，能不能請你稍等一下，好讓我能拿檔案？

❷ **Can you wait for ..., please? My colleague has a question.**（當別人有急事找你，需要暫停先處理時）
能不能請你稍等……？我同事有個問題。

例 Can you wait for a minute, please? My colleague has a question.
能不能請你稍等一分鐘？我同事有個問題。

❸ **Excuse me, (name). I have to ... Can you please wait ...?**
不好意思，（姓名）。我必須……。可以請你等……嗎？

例 Excuse me, Chris. I have to ask my <u>supervisor</u>. Can you please wait while I check with her?
不好意思，克里斯。我必須問我的上司。我跟她確認的時候可以請你等一下嗎？

❹ **(Name), I have to ... Can you wait ..., please?**
（姓名），我必須……。能請你等……嗎？

例 Roland, I have to check my records. Can you wait until I find the <u>transaction</u> you mentioned, please?
洛藍，我必須查一下我的紀錄。在我找到你說的那筆交易之前，能請你等一下嗎？

hold on *phr. v.*（電話）稍等；堅持
supervisor [ˌsupɚˋvaɪzɚ] *n.* 管理人；指導者
transaction [trænˋzækʃən] *n.* 交易；買賣

3.2 你需要更長的時間 You Need Longer than a Minute

如果你需要更長的時間，不方便讓對方在線上等待的話，可用下列四句告訴對方你將於稍後回電。

❶ Can I call you back in a couple of minutes? I have to check ...（當你需要查核資料時）

我能不能幾分鐘之後再打給你？我必須查對……。

例 Can I call you back in a couple of minutes, Scott? I have to check on these prices.

史考特，我能不能幾分鐘之後再打給你？我必須查對一下這些價格。

❷ Can you give me a couple of minutes and I'll call you back (as soon as/when) ...?（當你需要確定某事時）

你能不能給我幾分鐘的時間，我（一……／在……的時候）就回電給你？

例 Can you give me a couple of minutes and I'll call you back as soon as I get the answer.

你能不能給我幾分鐘的時間，我一得到答案就回電給你。

❸ Let me call you back right away. I have to (sort out/figure out/find out) ...（當你需要釐清某事時）

我馬上回電給你。我必須（釐清／想清楚／找出）……。

例 Let me call you back right away. I have to sort out a problem for one of my colleagues.

我馬上回電給你。我必須幫我一個同事釐清一個問題。

❹ (Name), I have ... I have to deal with. Can I call you back ...?（當需要處理的事情費時較長時）

（姓名），我有……必須處理。我能不能……回電給你？

例 Steve, I have an emergency I have to deal with. Can I call you back tomorrow?

史帝夫，我有個緊急情況必須處理。我能不能明天回電給你？

check on sth./sb. 檢查某物／某人（以確定他們相當安全或一切很好）
figure out *phr. v.* 想出；理解
emergency [ɪ`mɝdʒənsɪ] *n.* 緊急情況；突發事件

小心陷阱

☹ 錯誤用法

It's been good to **hear of** you. I'm glad we **reached agreement** on the **contract term**.

能接到你的電話真好。很高興我們就合約條件達成了協議。

☺ 正確用法

It's been good to **hear from** you. I'm glad we **reached an agreement** on the **contract requirements**.

能接到你的電話真好。很高興我們就合約條件達成了協議。

文化小叮嚀

Canadians are often considered to be more formal than Americans when it comes to using people's names and titles. Typically, you should address a Canadian customer using their last name and title until you are told otherwise. Interestingly, Western Canadians are considered less formal than their Eastern counterparts and are often quicker to move to a first name relationship.

談到使用人名和頭銜時，加拿大人常被認為比美國人注重形式。一般說來，你應該用姓氏和頭銜來稱呼一個加拿大客戶，直到你被告知可用其他方式為止。有趣的是，西部加拿大人被認為比他們的東岸同胞來得較不拘泥形式，也常較快進入直接稱呼名字的關係。

consider sb./sth. to be Adj./N. 認爲某人／某事物是……

when it comes to N./Ving 談到……；論及……

title [`taɪtḷ] *n.* 頭銜；稱號

typically [`tɪpɪkḷɪ] *adv.* 典型地；向來

address [ə`drɛs] *v.* 稱呼；對……說話

counterpart [`kaʊntɚ͵pɑrt] *n.* 對應的人（或物）；契約（副本）

4 實戰演練 Practice Exercises

I 請為下列三題選出最適本章的中文譯義。

1. hear from someone

   (A) 聽說某人的消息 (B) 聽到某人說話 (C) 獲得某人的電話或書信聯絡

2. reach an agreement on something

   (A) 完成某事的簽約 (B) 就某事達成協議 (C) 結束某事的合作

3. run something past somebody

   (A) 將某事告訴某人 (B) 將某物遞給某人 (C) 在某方面超越某人

II 請根據你聽到的內容為下列兩題選出正確解答。

1. What does the woman want?

   (A) To thank the man for his help.

   (B) To ask a few more questions.

   (C) To leave in a few minutes.

2. What will happen next?

   (A) The woman will make another appointment with the man.

   (B) The man will leave.

   (C) The woman will ask the man a few more questions.

III 電子郵件的效率眾所皆知，然而還是有很多人喜歡打電話聯絡，其中的原因之一就是感覺比較有「人味」。有時候，打電話給客戶的目的並不是要談什麼重要的事情，純粹只是為了聯絡感情；這樣的電訪的確有存在的必要，但要注意，千萬別讓它成為你常拿起話筒的原因。利用下列詞語模擬情境寫一篇會話，練習一下社交技巧吧。

haven't heard from you	touch base	ring
I just wanted	get going	that covers it

＊解答請見 228 頁

與你的客戶或同事共事

Working with Your Customers or Colleagues

untitled

Send Now | Send Later | Save as Draft | Add Attachments | Signature | Options | Rewrap

To: Wallace Kuo, Lucy Liao

From: Peter Chen

Default Font | Text Size

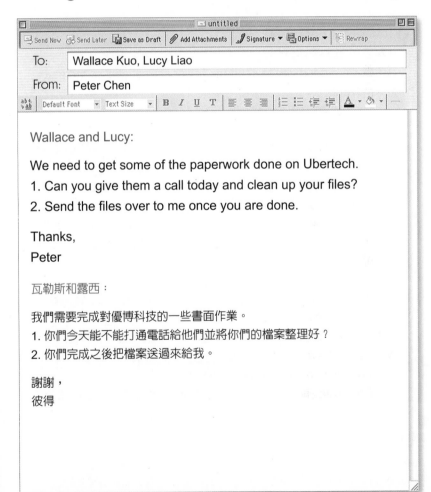

Wallace and Lucy:

We need to get some of the paperwork done on Ubertech.

1. Can you give them a call today and clean up your files?
2. Send the files over to me once you are done.

Thanks,
Peter

瓦勒斯和露西：

我們需要完成對優博科技的一些書面作業。

1. 你們今天能不能打通電話給他們並將你們的檔案整理好？
2. 你們完成之後把檔案送過來給我。

謝謝，
彼得

1 Biz 必通句型 Need-to-Know Phrases

1.1 指派任務 Introducing Tasks

CD I-30

「人心齊，泰山移」，懂得授權運用人力能大幅提昇工作效率；下列三句是語氣比較堅定的要求。

❶ (Name), I need you to ...

（姓名），我需要你……。

例 Collin, I need you to send me the specifications for the earth-movers.

柯林，我需要你把推土機的規格明細送來給我。

❷ (Name), we have to have ... before we can ... Can you get ... today?

（姓名），在我們能……之前，我們必須要有……。你今天能拿到……嗎？

例 Paul, we have to have the shipping details before we can book with the freight forwarder. Can you get those details today?

保羅，在我們能向貨運承攬商訂艙之前，我們必須要有出貨明細。你今天能拿到那些明細嗎？

❸ (Name), I haven't received ... yet. Can you send (it/them) as soon as ...?

（姓名），我還沒有收到……。你能不能一……就把（它／它們）送過來？

例 Hans, I haven't received the packing lists yet. Can you send them as soon as you get a chance?

漢斯，我還沒有收到包裝明細表。你能不能一有機會就把它們送過來？

Word List

earthmover [ˋɝθˏmuvɚ] *n.* 推土機；挖土機
book [bʊk] *v.* 預訂（座位、車票等）；登記
freight [fret] *n.* 貨物；運費
forwarder [ˋfɔrwɚdɚ] *n.* 運送者；運輸業者
packing list [ˋpækɪŋ ˏlɪst] *n.* 包裝明細表

下列五句的語氣較為婉轉。

❹ (Name), is it possible that you could send me ...?
（姓名），你有沒有可能可以把……送來給我？
例 Timothy, is it possible that you could send me the price list for consideration?
提莫西，你有沒有可能可以把價目表送來給我參考？

❺ (Name), what are the chances that you could ... by ...?
（姓名），你能在……以前……的可能性有多大？
例 Daniel, what are the chances that you could send the blueprint to the manufacturer by Wednesday?
丹尼爾，你能在星期三以前把藍圖送去給製造商的可能性有多大？

❻ I know this is a lot to ask, but we need ... ASAP.
我知道這樣要求太多，但是我們需要……，愈快愈好。
例 Sylvia, I know this is a lot to ask, but we need the contract signed ASAP.
絲薇亞，我知道這樣要求太多，但是我們需要合約完成簽名，愈快愈好。

❼ (Name), is there any chance that you can get me ... in the next couple of days?
（姓名），接下來的幾天內，你有可能可以給我……嗎？
例 Roland, is there any chance that you can get me the specs for the new wireless remotes in the next couple of days?
洛藍，接下來的幾天內，你有可能可以給我新型無線遙控器的規格明細嗎？

❽ Before ..., we are going to need ... Is it possible to get that done right away?
在……之前，我們需要……。有可能馬上完成這件事嗎？
例 Before we start production, we are going to need the order finalized. Is it possible to get that done right away?
在我們開始生產之前，我們需要將這份訂單定案。有可能馬上完成這件事嗎？

Word List

consideration [͵kənsɪdə`reʃən] *n.* 考慮；體諒

blueprint [`blu`prɪnt] *n.* 藍圖；設計圖

ASAP 儘快；愈快愈好（as soon as possible 的縮寫）

wireless [`waɪrlɪs] *adj.* 無線的

remote [rɪ`mot] *n.* 遙控器（remote control 的簡稱）

1.2 列出一張行動清單 Creating an Action List

清單的基本功用在於提醒，進階功用則在於增加動力；用下列八句列出一張專屬於你的行動清單吧。

❶ Let's go through ... again.
讓我們再把……看過一遍。

例 Let's go through this checklist again.
讓我們再把這張檢查表看過一遍。

❷ Let me get this straight. The first action item is ...
讓我把這個搞清楚。第一個行動項目是……。

例 Let me get this straight. The first action item is to finalize shipping arrangements.
讓我把這個搞清楚。第一個行動項目是將出貨安排定案。

❸ Let me get this straight. The first priority is ...
讓我把這個搞清楚。第一優先是……。

例 Let me get this straight. The first priority is to finalize product specifications.
讓我把這個搞清楚。第一優先是將產品規格定案。

❹ Can we recap the major points from our discussion? First, ... Is that right?
我們能不能簡扼重述一下我們討論的幾個重點？首先，……。對嗎？

例 Can we recap the major points from our discussion? First, we agreed to cover the postage and handling charge. Is that right?
我們能不能簡扼重述一下我們討論的幾個重點？首先，我們同意負擔郵資和手續費。對嗎？

Word List

go through *phr. v.* 檢視；審閱；經歷
checklist [`tʃɛk͵lɪst] *n.* 核對用的清單
Let me get this straight. 讓我把這個搞清楚。
item [`aɪtəm] *n.* 項目；條款
arrangements [ə`rendʒmənts] *n.*（通常複數）安排；準備
priority [praɪ`ɔrətɪ] *n.* 優先（權）
recap [ri`kæp] *v.* 重述重點
postage [`postɪdʒ] *n.* 郵資
handling charge [`hændlɪŋ ͵tʃɑrdʒ] *n.* 手續費

❺ Can we go through the list again? First, ... Second, ... And last, ...
我們能不能再把這份清單瀏覽一遍？第一，……。第二，……。最後，……。

例 Can we go through the list again? First, the <u>USB</u> memory sticks are one <u>gigabyte</u>. Second, you need 3,000 units. And last, you need them by February 9.
我們能不能再把這份清單瀏覽一遍？第一，USB 記憶卡是 1GB。第二，你們需要 3,000 張。最後，你們在二月九日以前要。

❻ I just want to take a minute and revisit ...
我想用一點時間重新檢視……。

例 I just want to take a minute and revisit the specifications for the LCD monitors you're interested in.
我想用一點時間重新檢視那些你有興趣的液晶螢幕的規格。

❼ If you don't mind, I'd like to go through ... to make sure that we are on the same page.
如果你不介意的話，我想查閱一下……，以確定我們的想法一致。

例 If you don't mind, I'd like to go through our contract for 2006 to make sure that we are on the same page.
如果你不介意的話，我想查閱一下我們 2006 年的合約，以確定我們的想法一致。

❽ Let me <u>summarize</u>. We agreed that ... Is that correct?
讓我做一下總結。我們同意……。正確嗎？

例 Let me summarize. We agreed that we are going to change the purchase <u>quantity</u> to 8,000 <u>sets</u>. Is that correct?
讓我做一下總結。我們同意將購買數量改為 8,000 組。正確嗎？

Word List

USB【電腦】通用序列匯流排（<u>U</u>niversal <u>S</u>erial <u>B</u>us 的縮寫，匯流排 Bus 是一組由金屬線構成的資訊傳輸線路）

gigabyte [ˋgɪgəˏbaɪt] *n.*【電腦】（記憶容量或資料的單位）十億位組；十億字節

summarize [ˋsʌməˏraɪz] *v.* 總結；概述

quantity [ˋkwɑntətɪ] *n.* 數量；量

set [sɛt] *n.* 一套；一副；一組

2 實戰會話 Show Time

CD I-31

2.1 Dialogue

Lucy needs Marie to send her the shipping details and first payment for Ubertech's order.

Lucy: Marie, I have two urgent requests.

Marie: OK. What can I do for you?

Lucy: Is there any chance that you can get me the shipping details in the next couple of days?

Marie: Sure, I don't think that would be a problem. What else can I do for you?

Lucy: I know this is a lot to ask, but we need the first payment ASAP. Before we start production, we are going to need the payment.

Marie: Well, that request will be a bit more difficult. I need two signatures on my end. Then I need to forward the payment to you, and that will take some time.

Lucy: Is there any chance that you can get me that payment in the next couple of days?

Marie: Well, I'll see what I can do. But I can't promise anything.

Lucy: Oh ... I appreciate your effort, Marie. Can you call me and let me know when you send the payment, so I can speed things up on my end?

譯文

露西需要瑪莉寄優博科技訂單的出貨明細及第一筆款項給她。

露西：瑪莉，我有兩個緊急要求。

瑪莉：好。我能替妳做什麼？

露西：接下來的幾天內，妳有可能可以給我出貨明細嗎？

瑪莉：當然，我不覺得這會是個問題。我還能幫妳做什麼？

露西：我知道這樣要求太多，但是我們需要頭款，愈快愈好。在我們開始生產之前，我們需要這筆款項。

瑪莉：呃，這個要求會比較困難一點。我這邊需要兩個人的簽名。然後我需要將款項轉給你們，那需要一些時間。

露西：接下來的幾天內，妳有可能可以給我那筆錢嗎？

瑪莉：嗯，我看我能做什麼，但我不能做任何保證。

露西：噢……我很感謝妳盡力，瑪莉。妳把錢匯出時能不能打電話讓我知道，好讓我加快我這邊的速度？

Word List

urgent [`ɝdʒənt] *adj.* 緊急的；急迫的
request [rɪ`kwɛst] *n./v.* 要求；請求
signature [`sɪgnətʃɚ] *n.* 簽名
on my end 我這邊；我這端
forward [`fɔrwɚd] *v.* 轉交；（電子郵件等）轉寄
appreciate [ə`priʃɪ͵et] *v.* 感謝；欣賞；意識到
speed up *phr. v.* 加速；增快

2.2 Dialogue

Wallace and Roland have made a final agreement on the card reader order. Now Wallace wants to recap the major points of their agreement.

Wallace: Can we recap the major points from our discussion? First, we agreed to increase the card reader order to 4,000 units. Is that right?

Roland: Correct. We changed the order from 3,000 units to 4,000 units.

Wallace: OK, great. Can we go through the list again? First, the order is increased. Second, the Ubertech logo is going on the side of the card reader. And last, you need the card readers by December 14th.

Roland: That's right. The only other issue is that they must be here no later than the 14th.

Wallace: I understand. I don't think that will be any problem. Our schedule is to have them to you prior to the 14th. Lucy has a couple of issues she wants to talk to you about. Can I pass you to her?

Roland: Sure, no problem.

Lucy: Hi, Roland. I just want to take a minute and revisit the shipping information. We agreed that the shipment would be FOB origin. Is that correct?

譯文

瓦勒斯和洛藍已經對讀卡機的訂單達成最後協議。現在瓦勒斯想要簡扼重述一下他們協議中的幾個重點。

瓦勒斯：我們能不能簡扼重述一下我們討論的幾個重點？首先，我們同意將讀卡機訂單增加為 4,000 部。對嗎？

洛藍： 沒錯。我們把訂單從 3,000 部改成 4,000 部。

瓦勒斯：好，很好。我們能不能再把這份清單瀏覽一遍？第一，訂單增加。第二，優博科技的商標會跑在讀卡機的側面。最後，你們十二月十四號以前要這批讀卡機。

洛藍： 沒錯。另外唯一要注意的問題是它們送達的時間一定不能晚於十四號。

瓦勒斯：我知道，我想那不會是個問題。我們的計劃是在十四號以前就把它們交給你們。露西有幾件事想跟你談。我可以把你轉過去給她嗎？

洛藍： 當然，沒問題。

露西：嗨，洛藍。我只是想用一點時間重新檢視一下出貨資料。我們同意貨運方式是 FOB 出貨點。對嗎？

Word List

make an agreement on sth. 對某事做成協議（agreement [əˋgrimənt] *n.*（可數）協議，協定；（不可數）同意）
no later than ... 不遲於……
prior to ... 在……以前

3 Biz 加分句型 Nice-to-Know Phrases

CD I-32

3.1 你的聯絡人即將／正在休假 Your Contact Is Taking a Holiday

未能於聯絡人休假或出差前妥善進行調度常是造成工作延遲的原因；當你知道連絡人即將離開工作崗位一段時間，別忘了提早安排並詢問是否有人可代爲處理。

① Is there any way we can ... before ...?（態度較和緩）
我們有沒有辦法能在……之前……？

例 Is there any way we can finalize shipping dates before Friday?
我們有沒有辦法能在星期五之前將出貨日期定案？

② You have to give me ... before ...（態度較堅決）
你必須在……之前給我……。

例 You have to give me the product specs before you take your holiday.
你必須在你休假之前給我產品規格。

③ Well, is there any possibility that ... can <u>take care of</u> this?（詢問某人是否可代為處理）
呃，有沒有可能……能處理這件事？

例 Well, is there any possibility that someone in shipping can take care of this?
呃，有沒有可能出貨部門的某個人能處理這件事？

④ We have to get this done. Who can I talk to?（尋找代理人）
我們必須把這件事搞定。我能夠找誰談？

例 We have to get this done. Since Greg is gone, who can I talk to?
我們必須把這件事搞定。既然葛瑞格不在，我能夠找誰談？

Word List

take care of sb./sth. 照顧某人；處理某事

3.2 你的客戶動怒了 Your Client Gets Angry

❶ Sorry, (name). I don't mean to be rude, but ...（道歉並解釋）

抱歉，(姓名)。我沒有不禮貌的意思，但……。

例 Sorry, Cynthia. I don't mean to be rude, but we won't meet our deadlines unless we get this done.

抱歉，欣希雅。我沒有不禮貌的意思，但如果這個不搞定的話，我們會趕不上期限。

❷ I'm just trying to ensure that ...（單純表示用意）

我只是想確保……。

例 I'm just trying to ensure that you get the product you want.

我只是想確保你能得到你要的產品。

❸ What I mean to say is ...（說明本意）

我想說的是……。

例 What I mean to say is that we absolutely have to resolve this issue.

我想說的是我們絕對得解決這個問題。

❹ Don't get me wrong. It's just that ...（柔性堅持）

不要誤會我的意思。只是……。

例 Don't get me wrong, Sylvia. It's just that we will miss our shipment dates if we don't finalize the new packaging design.

不要誤會我的意思，絲薇亞。只是如果我們不將新的包裝設計定案的話，我們會錯過出貨日期。

Word List

mean to V. 有做……的意思

rude [rud] *adj.* 無禮的；粗魯的

meet a deadline 趕上期限

resolve [rɪ`zɑlv] *v.* 解決；決定

Don't get me wrong. 別誤解我的意思。

小心陷阱

☹ 錯誤用法

If you **won't** mind, **I'll like** to revisit the lists.

如果你不介意的話，我想重新檢視一下那些清單。

☺ 正確用法

If you **don't** mind, **I'd like** to revisit the lists.

如果你不介意的話，我想重新檢視一下那些清單。

文化小叮嚀

Although only 5% of US college graduates speak a second language, Americans are likely to be interested in your culture. In fact, explaining interesting aspects of your culture is an excellent way to break down cultural barriers and develop a successful business relationship.

雖然只有 5% 的美國大學畢業生會說第二種語言，美國人很可能會對你的文化感興趣。事實上，解釋你的文化中有趣的層面是一個打破文化隔閡與建立成功商務關係的絕佳方式。

aspect [`æspɛkt] *n.* 方面；面貌

excellent [`ɛksələnt] *adj.* 優秀的；出色的

break down *phr .v.* 打破；故障；失敗

barrier [`bærɪɚ] *n.* 阻礙；障礙；路障

4 實戰演練 Practice Exercises

I 請為下列四題選出最適本章的中文譯義。

❶ a lot to ask

(A) 很多要問 (B) 要求過多 (C) 規矩太多

❷ Let me get this straight.

(A) 讓我坦白說出整件事情。 (B) 讓我好好解釋這件事情。 (C) 讓我把這件事搞清楚。

❸ no later than ...

(A) 最快於…… (B) 不遲於…… (C) 提早於……

❹ Don't get me wrong.

(A) 別搞混我。 (B) 別誤會我。 (C) 別害我。

II 根據你聽到的內容為下列兩題選出正確解答。

❶ What does the man want the woman to do?

(A) Change the color of the memory sticks.

(B) Contact the manufacturer.

(C) Change the product specs.

❷ What will the man and woman talk about next?

(A) Product specs.

(B) Color changes.

(C) Problems with the memory sticks.

III 談話結束前，你想列張行動清單記錄這次的工作要項，以便提醒自己。回想一下最近工作遇到的情況，利用下列詞語寫一篇短文訓練自己成為摘要高手吧。

go through	action item	first/second/third
shipping deadline	ASAP	

＊解答請見 230 頁

釐清問題
Sorting Out Problems

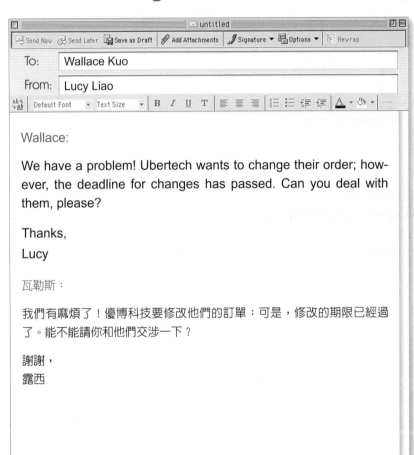

To: Wallace Kuo

From: Lucy Liao

Wallace:

We have a problem! Ubertech wants to change their order; however, the deadline for changes has passed. Can you deal with them, please?

Thanks,
Lucy

瓦勒斯：

我們有麻煩了！優博科技要修改他們的訂單；可是，修改的期限已經過了。能不能請你和他們交涉一下？

謝謝，
露西

1 Biz 必通句型 Need-to-Know Phrases

1.1 傳達變更 Communicating Changes

用下列三句來通知當事者有哪些事項需要改變。

❶ **(Name), we need to discuss changes to ...**
(姓名)，我們需要討論……的變更。
例 Wallace, we need to discuss changes to the order.
瓦勒斯，我們需要討論訂單的變更。

❷ **(Name), we have to make some changes to ...**
(姓名)，我們必須對……做些修改。
例 Roland, we have to make some changes to product packaging.
洛藍，我們必須對產品的包裝做些修改。

❸ **(Name), I'm sorry but we changed our minds about ...**
(姓名)，很抱歉，我們改變了我們對……所做的決定。
例 Wallace, I'm sorry but we changed our minds about the order size.
瓦勒斯，很抱歉，我們改變了我們對訂單數量所做的決定。

下列兩句用來詢問有哪些變動。

❹ **(Name), are there any changes to ... that I need to know about?**
(姓名)，有沒有任何關於……的變動是我需要知道的？
例 Roland, are there any changes to product features that I need to know about?
洛藍，有沒有任何關於產品特性的變動是我需要知道的？

❺ What exactly are the changes to ... that you want to make?

對於……，你（們）確切想做些什麼改變？

例 What exactly are the changes to the memory stick order that you want to make?

對於記憶卡訂單，你們確切想做些什麼改變？

最後三句用來拒絕或接受變更。

❻ I have to <u>check to see if</u> we can make changes to ... <u>at this point in time</u>.

我必須查一下確認我們這個時候是否還能對……做改變。

例 I have to check to see if we can make changes to the product specs at this point in time.

我必須查一下確認我們這個時候是否還能對產品規格做改變。

❼ I'm sorry, (name), but we can't change ... at this time. We have already ...

對不起，（姓名），這個時候我們不能更改……。我們已經……。

例 I'm sorry, Tania, but we can't change the <u>ingredients</u> at this time. We have already sent the order to our manufacturer.

對不起，坦妮雅，這個時候我們不能更改成分。我們已經將訂單送給我們的製造商了。

❽ If we change ..., it's going to <u>affect</u> ...

如果我們改變……的話，會影響到……。

例 If we change the specs, it's going to affect price.

如果我們改變規格的話，會影響到價格。

check to see if ... 查一下看看是否……

at this point in time 現在；此刻 (= at this point, at this moment)

ingredient [ɪn`gridɪənt] *n.* 成分；構成要素

affect [ə`fɛkt] *v.* 影響；對……發生作用

2.2 討論改變所造成的影響 Discussing the Effects of Changes

❶ Changes to ... are going to have a (marked/significant/considerable/substantial/dramatic) influence on ...
……的改變將對……造成（顯著的／重大的／相當的／實質的／劇烈的）的影響。

例 Changes to the components are going to have a significant influence on price.
零件的改變將對價格造成重大的影響。

❷ The changes to ... have had an unavoidable effect on ...
……的改變已經對……帶來不可避免的影響。

例 The changes to the trend have had an unavoidable effect on this season's net profit.
趨勢的改變已經對這一季的淨利帶來不可避免的影響。

❸ The ... changes have changed ...
……的改變已經改變了……。

例 The coating changes have subtly changed the colors as well as the entire product appearance.
塗層的改變已經微妙地改變了顏色和整個產品的外觀。

❹ We need to talk about adjustments to ...
我們需要談一下有關……的調整。

例 We need to talk about adjustments to our monthly retainer and to the commission we offer for each sale.
我們需要談一下有關我們每個月的約聘金，以及每筆交易我們所提供的佣金的調整。

Word List

marked [mɑrkt] *adj.* 顯著的
significant [sɪg`nɪfəkənt] *adj.* 重大的；重要的
considerable [kən`sɪdərəbl̩] *adj.* 相當多的
substantial [səb`stænʃəl] *adj.* 實質的；大量的
dramatic [drə`mætɪk] *adj.* 戲劇性的；不尋常的
component [kəm`ponənt] *n.* 零件；成分
unavoidable [͵ʌnə`vɔɪdəbl̩] *adj.* 不可避免的
net profit [`nɛt `prɑfɪt] *n.* 淨利
coating [`kotɪŋ] *n.* 塗層；外層
subtly [`sʌtl̩ɪ] *adv.* 微妙地；細微地
as well as 和；以及
adjustment [ə`ʤʌstmənt] *n.* 調整；修正
retainer [rɪ`tenɚ] *n.* 約聘金
commission [kə`mɪʃən] *n.* 佣金

5 As a result of ... modifications, we have to revisit ...

由於……的修改，我們必須重新討論……。

例 As a result of order modifications, we have to revisit our pricing policy for this client.

由於訂單的修改，我們必須重新討論對這位客戶的定價策略。

6 I'm trying to minimize the effect these ... changes will have on ...

我正試著把這些……的改變將對……造成的影響減到最低。

例 I'm trying to minimize the effect these process changes will have on quality and efficiency.

我正試著把這些流程的改變將對品質與效率造成的影響減到最低。

7 I've been able to cut a few corners to limit the effect on ...

我能在某些方面「做些調整」，把對……的影響控制在一定範圍之內。

例 I've been able to cut a few corners to limit the effect on operating expenses.

我能在某些方面「做些調整」，把對營運費用的影響控制在一定範圍之內。

8 If we ... I don't think there will be any effect on ...

如果我們……，我想並不會對……產生任何影響。

例 If we change the delivery date, I don't think there will be any effect on cost.

如果我們改變交貨日期，我想並不會對成本產生任何影響。

Word List

as a result of ... 由於……

modification [ˌmɑdəfəˋkeʃən] *n.* 修改；修正

price [praɪs] *v.* 訂定價格

minimize [ˋmɪnəˌmaɪz] *v.* 使……減到最小；使……減至最低

process [ˋprɑsɛs] *n.* 步驟；程序

efficiency [ɪˋfɪʃənsɪ] *n.* 效率；效能

cut corners 取巧；抄近路；（不照正常程序）用簡便方法做事

operating expenses [ˋɑpəretɪŋ ɪkˋspɛnsɪz] *n.* 營運費用

2 實戰會話 Show Time

2.1 Dialogue

Wallace and Roland sort out the changes to Ubertech's first order.

Roland: Wallace, I'm sorry but we changed our minds about the memory sticks.

Wallace: What exactly are the changes to the order that you want to make?

Roland: Well, we have decided to <u>go with</u> the complementary colors on the sticks.

Wallace: I'm going to have to check to see if we can make changes to the colors at this point in time. Just <u>hang on</u> for a second.

Wallace: I'm sorry Roland, but we can't change the colors at this time. We have already sent the order to our manufacturer and the order <u>is in production</u>.

Roland: Wallace, we have to change this. It's <u>out of my hands</u>. This change is from product development.

Wallace: If we change the memory stick color, it's going to affect price and shipment date.

Roland: As I said Wallace, it's <u>non-negotiable</u> on my end. You'll just have to let me know what it will mean <u>in terms of</u> cost and shipment date.

Wallace: OK. I'll see what I can do and <u>get back to</u> you.

譯文

瓦勒斯和洛藍整理出優博科技第一張訂單的變動。

洛藍：　瓦勒斯，很抱歉，我們改變了我們對記憶卡所做的決定。

瓦勒斯：對於訂單，你們確切想做什麼改變？

洛藍：　呃，我們已經決定記憶卡要選擇使用互補色。

瓦勒斯：我必須查一下確認我們這個時候是否還能對顏色做改變。稍等一下。

瓦勒斯：很抱歉，洛藍，這個時候我們不能更改顏色。我們已經將訂單送給我們的製造商了，而且訂單正在生產中。

洛藍：　瓦勒斯，我們一定要改。這不是我能掌控的。這個變動是產品開發部決定的。

瓦勒斯：如果我們改變記憶卡的顏色，會影響到價格和交貨日期。

洛藍：　就像我剛說的，瓦勒斯，我這邊沒有商量的餘地。你只需要讓我知道成本和送貨日期會受到什麼影響就好了。

瓦勒斯：好。我看我能做些什麼再打電話給你。

Word List

go with *phr. v.* 選擇使用；伴隨；與……相配
hang on *phr. v.* 稍待；堅持下去；緊握不放
be in production 生產中
(sth. is) out of one's hands（某事物）非某人可掌控的
non-negotiable [ˏnɑnnɪˋgoʃjəbl̩] *adj.* 無商量餘地的；不可轉讓的
in terms of ... 就……而論；在……方面
get back to sb. 回電、信給某人；再聯絡某人

2.2 Dialogue

Lucy talks to Marie about how changes to the memory stick order will affect cost and shipping.

Lucy: As a result of order modifications, we have to revisit cost and delivery date.

Marie: I know. Roland told me he changed the order. I've been expecting your call.

Lucy: Well, I'm trying to minimize the effect these changes are having on delivery date.

Marie: I realize that we told you that delivery date was important, but if the product cost increases, we might be forced to abandon the order.

Lucy: Hmm ... If we change delivery date, I don't think there will be an effect on cost.

Marie: I've been able to cut a few corners to limit the effect on cost. So, if we push the date back by one week, I think our problems will be solved.

Lucy: That sounds great. I hope this hasn't been too much trouble on your end.

Marie: No trouble at all. This is not the first time we've had to make a few changes midstream.

譯文

露西告訴瑪莉記憶卡訂單的改變將如何影響成本和運貨。

露西：由於訂單的修改，我們必須重新討論成本和交貨日期。

瑪莉：我知道。洛藍告訴我他改了訂單。我一直在等妳的電話。

露西：呃，我正試著把這些改變對交貨日期造成的影響減到最低。

瑪莉：我知道我們告訴過你們交貨日期很重要，但是如果產品的成本增加，我們可能會被迫放棄這份訂單。

露西：嗯……如果我們改變交貨日期，我想並不會對成本產生影響。

瑪莉：我能在某些方面「做些調整」，把對成本的影響控制在一定範圍之內。所以，如果我們把日期往後延一個禮拜，我想我們的問題就可以被解決。

露西：聽起來很棒。我希望這件事沒有造成你們那邊太多的麻煩。

瑪莉：一點也不麻煩。這已經不是我們第一次必須在中途做一些改變了。

Word List

realize [`rɪəˌlaɪz] *v.* 瞭解；領悟；實現
be forced to V. 被強迫……
abandon [ə`bændən] *v.* 放棄；中止；遺棄
push the date back 把日期往後延
solve [sɑlv] *v.* 解決；解答
midstream [`mɪdˌstrim] *adv./n.* 中途（地）

3 Biz 加分句型 Nice-to-Know Phrases

CD II-03

3.1 你的手機電池快沒電了 Your Cell Phone Battery Is Running Out

❶ I'm going to have to call you back when ... My battery is running out.

我將必須等……的時候再回電給你。我的電池快用完了。

例 I'm going to have to call you back when I get to the office. My battery is running out.

我將必須等我到辦公室的時候再回電給你。我的電池快用完了。

❷ I'm losing my battery. Can I call you back in (time period)?

我的電池快沒電了。我能不能過（時間長度）再打給你？

例 I'm losing my battery. Can I call you back in 10 minutes?

我的電池快沒電了。我能不能過 10 分鐘再打給你？

❸ My battery is going/dying. I'll have to call you back ...

我的電池快沒了。我必須……再打給你。

例 My battery is going. I'll have to call you back tomorrow.

我的電池快沒了。我必須明天再打給你。

❹ I'm going to lose my battery. I'll call you back as soon as ...

我的電池就快沒電了。等我一……就回電給你。

例 I'm going to lose my battery. I'll call you back as soon as I get a chance.

我的電池就快沒電了。等我一有機會就回電給你。

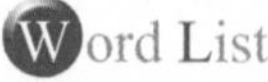

Word List

run out *phr. v.* 用完；逾期

get to (a place) 抵達（一個地方）

3.2 信號漸失 Losing the Signal

❶ I can't hear you. Can you repeat that? I'm losing my signal.（信號逐漸減弱）

我聽不到。你可不可以再說一次？我的訊號快消失了。

例 Hello? I can't hear you. Can you repeat that? Can you hear me? I'm losing my signal.

喂？我聽不到。你可不可以再說一次？你聽得見我嗎？我的訊號快消失了。

❷ My signal is going. I'll have to call you back.（告訴對方將再連絡）

我的訊號快沒了。我將必須再打電話給你。

例 Can you still hear me? My signal is going. I'll have to call you back when I get back to the office.

你還能聽得見我嗎？我的訊號快沒了。我將必須等我到辦公室的時候再打電話給你。

❸ My signal is getting weak. Let me call you back when ...（預告回電的時間）

我的訊號愈來愈弱。等……的時候，我再回電給你。

例 My signal is getting weak. Let me call you back when I return to the office.

我的訊號愈來愈弱。等回到辦公室的時候，我再回電給你。

❹ I'm coming to a long tunnel. I'll call you back ...（即將接近收訊不良的區域時）

我要進入一條長隧道了。……我再回電給你。

例 I'm coming to a long tunnel. I'll call you back on the other side.

我要進入一條長隧道了。到另一頭我再回電給你。

Did you know? 當你疲於和麻煩的客戶溝通時，也可以用以上這些句子來巧妙告退。謹記！不可露出不耐的口氣，同樣的說法亦應避免反覆使用，以免留下不良商譽。

signal [`sɪgn!] *n.* 信號；標誌；表示

tunnel [`tʌn!] *n.* 隧道；地道

小心陷阱

☹ 錯誤用法

I **must to** check to see **can we** make changes to the colors at this point **on** time.

我必須查一下確認我們這個時候是否還能對顏色做改變。

☺ 正確用法

I **have to** check to see **if we can** make changes to the colors at this point **in** time.

我必須查一下確認我們這個時候是否還能對顏色做改變。

文化小叮嚀

In the global business environment, companies are expected to research a market's culture, etiquette and business practices before entering that market. In fact, most international business experts cite lack of this knowledge as a major contributor to failure.

處於全球化的經濟環境，企業在進入市場之前都應該先調查一下該市場的文化、行規和做法。事實上，多數的國際企業專家都指出缺乏這個認知是造成失敗的一大主因。

Word List

be expected to V. 被期待做……；被寄望做……

etiquette [`ɛtɪkɛt] *n.*（業界的）規矩、行爲規範；禮儀

practice [`præktɪs] *n.* 實行；常規；（醫生、律師等專業人士的）執業

expert [`ɛkspɚt] *n.* 專家；能手

cite [saɪt] *v.* 舉出；引用

contributor [kən`trɪbjutɚ] *n.* 促成因素；捐獻者

4 實戰演練 Practice Exercises

I 請為下列四題選出最適本章的中文譯義。

❶ as a result of ...

(A) 因為…… (B) 所以…… (C) 結果……

❷ cut corners

(A) 智取 (B) 速戰速決 (C) 取巧

❸ out of one's hands

(A) 由某人所完成 (B) 由某人所促成 (C) 非某人可掌控

❹ push ... back

(A) 追溯…… (B) 把……往後延 (C) 回到……

II 請根據你聽到的內容為下列兩題選出正確解答。

❶ What aspect of the order does Paul want to change?

(A) The number of chips.

(B) The color of the product.

(C) The size of the chips.

❷ How many 512 GB chips does Paul want to order?

(A) 10,000.

(B) 20,000.

(C) 5,000.

III 為了達成預定目標，妥善溝通並清楚傳達所做的變更及可能造成的影響非常重要。有道是「牽一髮而動全身」，別讓小小的改變造成不可挽回的損失。打電話給客戶之前，利用下列詞語寫一篇短文練習一下吧。

revisit	as a result of	change their minds
modify	minimize	pricing policy

＊解答請見 232 頁

闡明議題
Clarifying Issues

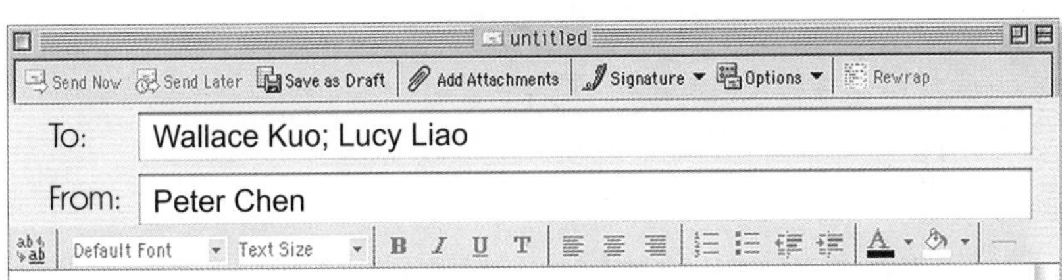

Wallace:

We still don't have an answer on the memory sticks. Get a final answer today!

Lucy:

You'll have to call Ubertech today. There seems to be some confusion over our agreement with them. Please find out what the problem is and resolve it.

Peter

瓦勒斯：

我們還是沒得到關於記憶卡的答覆。今天得要到一個確切的答案！

露西：

妳今天必須打電話給優博科技。我們和他們的協議似乎有一些混淆不清的地方。請找出問題在哪並把它解決掉。

彼得

1 Biz 必通句型 Need-to-Know Phrases

1.1 釐清訊息 Cleaning Up Communication

CD II-05

洽商時，如果有聽不懂或不確定對方所指何意的情況發生時，應該想辦法問清楚。含糊將就可能會釀出麻煩，未達共識的合作容易產生問題。

❶ (Name), I'm not sure what you mean by ...
（姓名），我不確定你說的……是什麼意思。

例 Roland, I'm not sure what you mean by dominant blue.
洛藍，我不確定你說的主藍色是什麼意思。

❷ (Name), can you clarify what you mean by ...?
（姓名），你能不能講清楚你說的……是什麼意思？

例 Roland, can you clarify what you mean by possible schedule changes?
洛藍，你能不能講清楚你說的進度表可能會變動是什麼意思？

❸ (Unclear word/statement)? What do you mean by (unclear word/statement)?
（不清楚的字／敘述）？你說（不清楚的字／敘述）是什麼意思？

例 Out-of-pocket expenses? What do you mean by out-of-pocket expenses?
代墊付費用？你說代墊付費用是什麼意思？

❹ (Name), I don't understand what you mean by ...
（姓名），我不懂你說的……是什麼意思。

例 Roland, I don't understand what you mean by unauthorized modifications.
洛藍，我不懂你說的未經授權的修改是什麼意思。

Word List

clean up *phr. v.* 整理；清理
dominant [`dɑmənənt] *adj.* 最顯著的；支配的
clarify [`klærə͵faɪ] *v.* 闡明；澄清
statement [`stetmənt] *n.* 陳述；（正式的）聲明
out-of-pocket expenses [`aʊtəv `pɑkɪt ɪk`spɛnsɪz] *n.* 代墊付費用；自掏腰包的開支（先代爲支付，通常於稍後領回）
unauthorized [͵ʌn`ɔθə͵raɪzd] *adj.* 未被授權的；未經許可的

❺ (Name), I'm a bit confused. I thought we already agreed ...

（姓名），我有一點搞混了。我以為我們已經同意……。

例 Wallace, I'm a bit confused. I thought we already agreed that we were going to change the production schedule.

瓦勒斯，我有一點搞混了。我以為我們已經同意我們要改變生產進度表。

❻ As I recall, you told me ...

我記得你告訴過我，……。

例 As I recall, you told me we had to change the colors.

我記得你告訴過我，我們必須改變顏色。

❼ My notes indicate that we agreed on ...

我的筆記寫說我們同意……。

例 My notes indicate that we had agreed on a complementary color scheme.

我的筆記寫說我們同意互補的配色方案。

❽ Sorry. I mean that the (position) hadn't signed off on ...

對不起。我的意思是（職位）還沒簽核……。

例 Sorry. I mean that the manager hadn't signed off on the changes.

對不起。我的意思是經理還沒簽核這些變動。

confused [kən`fjuzd] *adj.* 困惑的；混亂的

recall [rɪ`kɔl] *v.* 記得；回想；使……想起

indicate [`ɪndə͵ket] *v.* 指示；表明

color scheme [`kʌlɚ ͵skim] *n.* 配色方案；色調搭配

sign off on sth. 核准某事物

1.2 討論變更的影響 Discussing Effects of Changes

「配合變動做了一連串修改，但稍後又被告知維持原議即可」這樣白忙一場的情況偶爾會發生；此時，除了平心檢視整體所造成的影響，別忘了使用下列八句來釐清、確定對方的最終決定，以免再生枝節。

❶ What (issues) are you talking about?
你說的是什麼（議題）？

例 What changes are you talking about?
你說的是什麼變動？

❷ So, you mean that we are not going to ...
所以，你的意思是我們將不會……。

例 So, you mean that we are not going to go with the original component mix.
所以，你的意思是我們將不會選擇原來的零件組合。

❸ Then we won't have to change ...
那麼我們就不用更改……。

例 Then we won't have to change the delivery date.
那麼我們就不用更改交貨日期。

❹ Then there won't be any impact on ...
那麼對……就不會有任何影響。

例 Then there won't be any impact on cost.
那麼對成本就不會有任何影響。

original [ə`rɪdʒənl] *adj.* 原始的；原創的
mix [mɪks] *n./v.* 混合；搭配

❺ I see. We are going to ignore our previous conversation about ...

我懂了。我們就不用管我們先前關於……的對話。

例 I see. We are going to ignore our previous conversation about changing the insurance coverage.

我懂了。我們就不用管我們先前關於更改保險範圍的對話。

❻ So there won't be any changes to ..., correct?

所以……不會有任何改變，對嗎？

例 So there won't be any changes to the tax breaks we will receive, correct?

所以我們將獲得的稅金寬減額不會有任何改變，對嗎？

❼ What you are saying is that this (will/will not) affect ...?

你是說這（會／不會）影響……？

例 What you are saying is that this will not affect total cost?

你是說這不會影響總成本？

❽ I think I understand. Let me repeat this back to you. ... will remain the same.

我想我瞭解了。讓我向你重複一次。……將維持不變。

例 I think I understand. Let me repeat this back to you. The colors we will use are teal blue, and black and white, and the production run and delivery deadline will remain the same.

我想我瞭解了。讓我向你重複一次。我們將使用的顏色是藍綠色和黑白，生產數量和交貨期限將維持不變。

ignore [ɪg`nor] *v.* 忽視；不顧
coverage [`kʌvərɪdʒ] *n.* 保險項目（或範圍）；涵蓋範圍
tax break [`tæks ˏbrek] *n.* 稅金寬減額；賦稅減免（法定限額內所減免的費用，為優惠特定對象）
remain [rɪ`men] *v.* 保持；繼續存在
run [rʌn] *n.*（一次的）生產量

2 實戰會話 Show Time

2.1 Dialogue

When it comes time for final agreement, Roland and Wallace find that their communication is breaking down in an already complicated discussion.

Wallace: Hi, Roland. I need to get a final decision on this order.

Roland: No problem. We decided to go with dominant blue.

Wallace: Roland, I don't understand what you mean by dominant blue.

Roland: Well, as I mentioned before, our product color is teal blue.

Wallace: Roland, I'm a bit confused. I thought we had already agreed that you were going to go with complementary colors. As I recall, you told me that we had to change the color.

Roland: I know. I'm sorry. The marketing department didn't get clearance for the change.

Wallace: Clearance? What do you mean by clearance?

Roland: Sorry. I mean that the manager hadn't signed off on the change.

Wallace: OK. I think I understand. But let me confirm. We are not going with complementary colors. We are returning to our original plan–a teal blue, and black and white color scheme.

Roland: Right. It's my fault. I'm sorry for all this confusion.

譯文

到了要做最後協議的時候，洛藍和瓦勒斯發現他們的溝通在已經夠複雜的討論中出現了障礙。

瓦勒斯：喂，洛藍。我需要得到這份訂單的最後決定。

洛藍：　沒問題。我們決定選用主藍色。

瓦勒斯：洛藍，我不懂你說的主藍色是什麼意思。

洛藍：　呃，像我之前提過的，我們的產品顏色是藍綠色。

瓦勒斯：洛藍，我有一點搞混了。我以為我們已經同意你們要選用互補色。我記得你告訴過我，我們必須改變顏色。

洛藍：　我知道。很抱歉。行銷部並沒有獲得變更的許可。

瓦勒斯：許可？你說的許可是什麼意思？

洛藍：　抱歉。我的意思是經理還沒簽核這項變動。

瓦勒斯：好。我想我瞭解了。但讓我確認一下。我們將不會選用互補色。我們會回到我們原來的計劃——藍綠色和黑白的配色方案。

洛藍：　對。是我的錯。對於這一切的混亂我感到非常抱歉。

Word List

when it comes time for N. 到了要做……的時候
break down *phr .v.* 失敗；故障；分解
clearance [`klırəns] *n.* 許可（get clearance for N. 獲得……的許可）
confirm [kən`fɝm] *v.* 確認；證實

2.2 Dialogue

Lucy is not very happy. She needs to call Marie and redress product delivery dates and cost.

Lucy: Hi, Marie. I suspect that you've heard about the recent changes.

Marie: No, I haven't heard. What changes are you talking about?

Lucy: Well, that's the thing. There are no changes.

Marie: OK. You've lost me. Can you explain what you mean by "no changes"?

Lucy: Yes. The original plan for the color scheme–teal blue, and black and white–that's what we are going to use on the memory sticks.

Marie: So, you mean that we are not going with complementary colors.

Lucy: Correct.

Marie: Then we won't have to change the delivery date.

Lucy: Correct.

Marie: Then there won't be any impact on cost.

Lucy: Correct.

Marie: I see. We are going to ignore our previous conversation about changing delivery date and cost implications. Is that what you mean?

Lucy: You got it.

譯文

露西不是很高興。她需要打電話給瑪莉修正產品交貨日期和成本。

露西：喂，瑪莉。我想妳應該聽說了最近的變動。

瑪莉：沒有，我還沒聽說。妳說的是什麼變動？

露西：呃，這就是關鍵。沒有變動。

瑪莉：好。妳把我搞糊塗了。妳能不能解釋一下妳說的「沒有變動」是什麼意思？

露西：好。原來計劃的配色方案——藍綠色和黑白——是我們要用在記憶卡上的顏色。

瑪莉：所以，妳的意思是我們不會選用互補色？

露西：沒錯。

瑪莉：那我們就不用更改出貨日期。

露西：沒錯。

瑪莉：那對成本就不會造成任何影響。

露西：沒錯。

瑪莉：我懂了。我們就不用管我們之前關於改變交貨日期和成本可能會有影響的對話。妳是這個意思嗎？

露西：妳說對了。

Word List

redress [rɪ`drɛs] *v.* 修正；補救
suspect [sə`spɛkt] *v.* 懷疑；覺得……可能是事實；覺得可疑
That's the thing. 那就是關鍵。 那就是重點。
You've lost me. 你把我搞糊塗了。
implications [ˌɪmplɪ`keʃənz] *n.*（通常複數）可能產生的影響或結果
You got it. 你說對了。 你懂了。

3 Biz 加分句型 Nice-to-Know Phrases

3.1 你有插播時 You've Got Another Call

電話插播是一種既聰明又無禮的發明，聰明的是受話者可以依輕重緩急接聽電話處理事情；無禮的是原始來電者的談話受到打擾，沒有獲得「優先辦理」的尊重。使用下列四句讓自己有禮且得宜地處理插播。

❶ I'm sorry. Can you hold for a second?（發現有插播時請對方稍等）

對不起，您可以稍等一下嗎？

例 I'm sorry. I have another call that I need to take right away. Can you hold for a second?

對不起，我有另一通電話需要馬上接。你可以稍等一下嗎？

❷ I've got another call. Can I ...?（告訴對方有插播）

我有插播。我可以……嗎？

例 Excuse me. I've got another call. Can I call you back?

不好意思。我有插播。我可以再回電給你嗎？

❸ I'm going to have to call you back. Is (time) OK?（選擇中斷原先的談話，並詢問適合回電的時間）

我必須再回電給您。（時間）可以嗎？

例 I'm sorry, Gretchen. I'm going to have to call you back. Is 5:00 OK?

對不起，葛瑞倩。我必須再回電給妳。五點可以嗎？

❹ Can you hold while I ...?（請對方稍等）

您可不可以稍等，我……？

例 Can you hold while I take another call real quick, Tania? It shouldn't be more than a minute.

坦妮雅，妳可不可以稍等，我很快接一下另一通電話？應該不會超過一分鐘。

3.2 當你需要更多時間時 When You Need More Time

❶ **(Name), sorry about that. Can I call you back in (time period)?**（當對方已經在線上等了一段時間，而你不想讓他／她繼續等時）

（姓名），很抱歉讓您等候。我可以過（時間長度）再回電給您嗎？

例 Tania, sorry about that. Can I call you back in 10 minutes?

坦妮雅，很抱歉讓妳等候。我可以過 10 分鐘再回電給妳嗎？

❷ **(Name), my apologies. Do you mind if I call you back when ...?**（詢問對方某個時刻回電是否恰當）

（姓名），很抱歉。您介不介意我……的時候再回電給您？

例 David, my apologies. Do you mind if I call you back when I finish the conversation with the customer?

大衛，很抱歉。你介不介意我結束和客戶的對話後再回電給你？

❸ **(Name), I'm very sorry to keep you waiting. Is it OK if I call you back ...?**

（姓名），很抱歉讓您等候。我……再回電給您可以嗎?

例 Hans, I'm very sorry to keep you waiting. Is it OK if I call you back in a couple of minutes?

漢斯，很抱歉讓你等候。我過幾分鐘再回電給你可以嗎？

❹ **This call is going to take longer than I thought. Can I call you back ...?**

這通電話將比我預期的還要長。我能不能……再回電給您？

例 This call is going to take longer than I thought. Can I call you back this afternoon?

這通電話將比我預期的還要長。我能不能今天下午再回電給你？

apology [ə`pɑlədʒɪ] *n.* 道歉；陪罪

小心陷阱

☹ 錯誤用法

Roland, I'm **a bit of confusing**. I **thinked** we **have** already agreed to go with **complimentary** colors.

洛藍，我有一點搞混了。我以為我們已經同意選擇使用互補色。

☺ 正確用法

Roland, I'm **a bit confused**. I **thought** that we **had** already agreed to go with **complementary** colors.

洛藍，我有一點搞混了。我以為我們已經同意選擇使用互補色。

文化小叮嚀

It may seem strange that with emphasis placed on effective communication, lack of communication is a leading cause of misunderstanding, disagreement, and even partnership break-up. According to cross-cultural communication experts, you can't assume that an employee at your level in a foreign country has the same access to information as you, can speak as freely, or has the same authority when it comes to making decisions.

在有效溝通倍受重視之際，奇怪的是缺乏溝通仍是造成誤會、爭執，甚至是導致合作關係破裂的一個主要原因。根據跨文化溝通專家的說法，你不能預設一個在外國與你同等級的員工能和你一樣獲得資訊，能和你一樣暢所欲言，或是在做決定的時候能擁有和你一樣的權力。

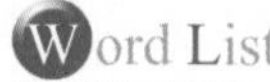

place emphasis on N. 強調……；重視……

leading [`lidɪŋ] *adj.* 主要的；領導的

disagreement [ˏdɪsə`grimənt] *n.* 意見不一；爭論

partnership [`pɑrtnɚˏʃɪp] *n.* 合夥關係

break-up *n.* 解散；分離；斷絕

cross- [`krɔs] *pref.* 跨……；橫過……

authority [ə`θɔrətɪ] *n.* 權力；權威

4 Practice Exercises 實戰演練

I 請為下列三題選出最適本章的中文譯義。

❶ clean up

(A) 釐清 (B) 終結 (C) 淨化

❷ sign off on ...

(A) 離開…… (B) 終止…… (C) 核准……

❸ You have lost me.

(A) 你忘了我。 (B) 你害我迷路。 (C) 你把我搞糊塗了。

II 請根據你聽到的內容為下列兩題選出正確解答。

❶ What part of the order will change?

(A) The product style.

(B) The product quantity.

(C) The delivery date.

❷ What did the man mean when he said "no changes"?

(A) He meant there would be absolutely no changes to the order.

(B) He meant that certain parts of the order wouldn't change.

(C) He meant that the cost would change, but the delivery date would not.

III 客戶告訴你他們的決定了，謹慎起見，你習慣複誦一次聽到的內容以確定自己沒有聽錯。利用下列詞語模擬情境，寫一篇短文為聽寫功夫打底吧。

repeat	make sure	mistake
clarify	I'm a bit confused	as I recall

＊解答請見 234 頁

解決問題
Solving Problems

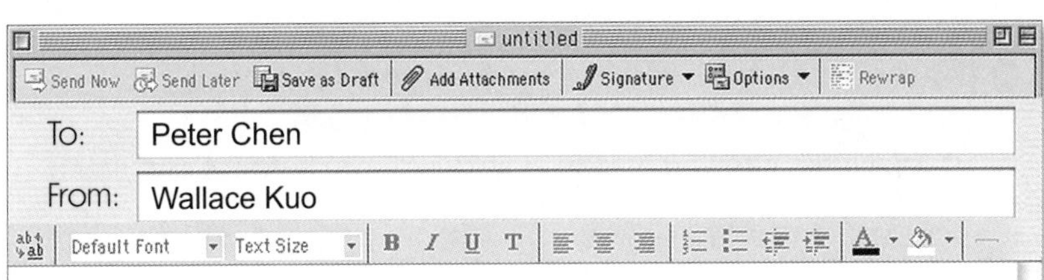

Peter:

We are in big trouble! I got a fax from Roland this morning, saying they need to change the colors. Can we have a meeting to discuss this?

Wallace
Sales Manager
Omega Electronics, Taiwan

彼得：

我們麻煩大了！我今天早上收到一張洛藍的傳真，說他們需要修改顏色。我們能開會討論一下這件事嗎？

瓦勒斯
台灣歐美嘉電子業務經理

1 Biz 必通句型 Need-to-Know Phrases

1.1 瞭解問題 Understanding Problems

CD II-09

發生狀況時，有些人的情緒很容易激動；此時，必須要有一方保持冷靜，以免場面愈演愈烈。下列兩句話用來緩和緊張的氣氛，並詢問事情的癥結所在。

❶ (Name), can you please slow down? I'm sure ...
（姓名），能不能請您稍微冷靜一下、不要急？我確定……。

例 Mr. Hung, can you please slow down? I'm sure we can find a solution.
洪先生，能不能請您稍微冷靜一下、不要急？我確定我們能找到解決方式。

❷ (Name), what exactly is the problem?
（姓名），究竟有什麼問題？

例 Chris, what exactly is the problem?
克里斯，究竟有什麼問題？

用下列兩句話告訴對方你能理解。

❸ Yes, (name), I'll talk to (person) to see if ... is possible.
是，（姓名），我會跟（某人）講，看有沒有可能……。

例 Yes, Hans, I'll talk to my manager to see if reducing the fee is possible.
是，漢斯，我會跟我的經理講，看有沒有可能把費用減少。

❹ Yes, I understand, (name). I hope ...
是的，（姓名），我瞭解。我希望……。

例 Yes, I understand, Cynthia. I hope we can work out the best way to minimize the damage.
是的，欣希雅，我瞭解。我希望我們能找出將損失降到最低的最好辦法。

Word List

slow down *phr. v.*（行動）放慢下來；減速
solution [sə`luʃən] *n.* 解答；解決辦法
fee [fi] *n.*（爲了使用或獲得服務所支付的）費用
work out *phr. v.* 找出；算出；理解；有好結果

即使是記性極佳的人遇到很多事情一起發生，也難保不會把一些細節搞混。能保持做筆記的習慣是好的，不僅可避免犯錯，日後如發生糾紛時也可以用來佐證。

❺ (Name), let me <u>go over</u> ... as I write it/them down.

（姓名），在我把它／它們寫下來的同時，讓我檢視一下……。

例 Sylvia, let me go over your request as I write it down.

絲薇亞，在我把它寫下來的同時，讓我檢視一下妳的要求。

❻ (Name), are there any <u>alternatives</u> to ... that are suitable?

（姓名），有任何適合的選擇可以取代……嗎？

例 Roland, are there any alternatives to our current <u>insurer</u> that are suitable?

洛藍，有任何適合的選擇可以取代我們目前的保險公司嗎？

❼ (Name), I'm not sure we can <u>accommodate</u> ...

（姓名），我不確定我們是否能因應……。

例 Roland, I'm not sure we can accommodate your requested change to the shipping schedule.

洛藍，我不確定我們是否能因應你們改變出貨時程的要求。

別無他法時，只好搬出白紙黑字的文件來證明。

❽ (Name), the (contract/agreement) <u>states</u> very clearly that ...

（姓名），（合約／協議書）上說的非常清楚，……。

例 Roland, the contract states very clearly that any changes to the order will <u>be subject to</u> additional costs.

洛藍，合約上說的非常清楚，訂單如有任何改變都需要附加費用。

go over sth. 察看某物；複習某物
alternative [ɔl`tɝnətɪv] *n.* 選擇；替代方法
insurer [ɪn`ʃʊrɚ] *n.* 保險公司；保險業者
accommodate [ə`kɑmə͵det] *v.* 適應；通融
state [stet] *v.* 陳述；聲明發生
be subject to sth. 以某事物爲條件；受某事物的支配或影響

1.2 取得共識 Obtaining Agreement

很多最終決定都是經過一番拉鋸後形成的；當情況僵持不下時，可用下列八句主動提議爭取先機。

❶ Is it possible that you can agree to ...?
你們有沒有可能同意……？

例 Is it possible that you can agree to pay half of the change fee?
你們有沒有可能同意支付一半的變更費用？

❷ Can you agree to ...?
你們能不能同意……？

例 Can you agree to not changing the colors but reducing the price of the original order instead?
你們能不能同意不改顏色，但是原本的訂單價格降低？

❸ What if we decided to ...? Would that work?
如果我們決定……呢？這樣可行嗎？

例 What if we decided to charge only 50% of the change penalty and reduce the shipping fee by 10%? Would that work?
如果我們決定只收 50% 的修改罰款，將運費減少 10% 呢？這樣可行嗎？

❹ Say we ... but/and then ... Would that be a suitable solution?
如果說我們……，但是／然後……。這會是個合適的解決辦法嗎？

例 Say we waive the change penalty but push the shipping date back by one month. Would that be a suitable solution?
如果說我們放棄修改罰款，但是把出貨日期往後延一個月。這會是個合適的解決辦法嗎？

agree to N./to do sth. 同意……；接受……
work [wɝk] *v.* 行得通；起作用
charge [ʧɑrʤ] *v.* 對……索費；指控
say ... 如果說……；比方說……
waive [wev] *v.* 放棄；撤回

❺ I know that this isn't exactly what you want, but what if we ...

我知道這不完全是你們想要的，但如果我們……呢？

例 I know that this isn't exactly what you want, but what if we made the change, but pushed the shipping date back by two weeks?

我知道這不完全是你們想要的，但如果我們做了修改，但把出貨日期往後延兩個禮拜呢？

❻ What is the most important (factor/issue) for you? Is it ...?

對你們來說最重要的（因素／議題）是什麼？是……嗎？

例 This is a complicated situation. What is the most important factor for you? Is it the color change?

這是個複雜的情況。對你們來說最重要的因素是什麼？是改變顏色嗎？

❼ Let's say that we ... Then we can ...

如果說我們……，那我們就能……。

例 Let's say that we delay shipping by two weeks. Then we can reduce the penalty.

如果說我們延遲兩個禮拜出貨，那我們就能減少罰款。

❽ The best I can do is ... I just don't have any more room to move.

我能做的最多就是……。我實在沒有周旋的空間了。

例 The best I can do is to cut the penalty by 50%. I just don't have any more room to move.

我能做的最多就是把罰款減半。我實在沒有周旋的空間了。

let's say ... 譬如說……；如果說……(= say ...)

room [rum] *n.* 空間；餘地

2 實戰會話 Show Time

2.1 Dialogue

Wallace doesn't like customers changing orders. He prefers such issues to be resolved prior to signing a contract.

Wallace: Roland, I realize that this color change is extremely important.

Roland: Look, Wallace. I'm under a lot of pressure. We have to change the order. But if there are extra costs, that will eat into our profit.

Wallace: Yes, I understand, Roland. I hope we can find a solution. Let me go over your request as I write it down. ... Roland, are there any alternatives to changing the memory stick colors that are suitable?

Roland: Well, not really. I suppose we have two problems. We need the color changed, and we have a problem with the extra charge for making the change.

Wallace: Roland, the contract states very clearly that any changes to the order will be subject to additional costs. And this is the second time we've changed the color scheme.

Roland: You're right, Wallace. But that doesn't really change things.

Wallace: OK, Roland. I'll talk to the president to see if reducing the fee is possible.

瓦勒斯不喜歡客戶修改訂單。他認為這種事在簽約前解決比較好。

瓦勒斯：洛藍，我瞭解這項顏色的變更非常重要。

洛藍：　聽著，瓦勒斯。我處於極大的壓力之下。我們必須修改訂單。但是如果得付額外的費用，那會損及我們的利潤。

瓦勒斯：是的，洛藍，我瞭解。我希望我們能找出一個解決辦法。在我寫下來的同時，讓我檢視一下你的要求。……洛藍，有任何適合的選擇可以取代改變記憶卡的顏色嗎？

洛藍：　嗯，好像沒有。我想我們有兩個問題。顏色我們需要改變，而且我們不能同意改變顏色所需的額外費用。

瓦勒斯：洛藍，合約上說的非常清楚，訂單如有任何改變都需要附加費用。而且這是我們第二次更改配色方案了。

洛藍：　你說的沒錯，瓦勒斯。但是那樣並沒有真的改變什麼。

瓦勒斯：好吧，洛藍。我會跟總裁講，看有沒有可能把費用減少。

Word List

resolve [rɪ`zɑlv] *v.* 解決；決定
extremely [ɪk`strimlɪ] *adv.* 極其；非常
be under pressure 處於壓力之下
extra [`ɛkstrə] *adj.* 額外的；附加的
eat into *phr. v.* 耗用一部分；侵蝕
suppose [sə`poz] *v.* 猜想；認爲
have a problem with sth. 不能同意某事

2.2 Dialogue

Lucy, Wallace and the president of Omega Electronics have a conference call to sort out the problem with Ubertech.

Lucy: What if we decided to waive the penalty fee? Would that work?

President: No, we can't do that. The penalty fee covers our cost in making a change.

Wallace: Well, what if we decided to waive the penalty fee and move the shipping date back by two weeks?

President: Sure, that would work for Ubertech. But we'll be stuck holding their order.

Lucy: Let's say that we waive 50% of the penalty, and write the cost into their next order. Then we won't lose anything in the long term and also keep a good customer.

Wallace: We'd also be showing them that we are willing to do our best to meet their needs.

President: Well, do you two really believe that Ubertech is going to be a good customer in the long term?

Wallace: Sure, I've developed a good relationship with Roland. Let's say that we cut the penalty by 50%. Then we can add it to their future contracts. I think it's a win-win solution, and I think that I can sell it to Roland.

譯文

露西、瓦勒斯和歐美嘉電子總裁開了一場電話會議來釐清和優博科技的問題。

露西： 如果我們決定放棄懲罰費用呢？這樣可行嗎？

總裁： 不，我們不能那麼做。懲罰費用包括我們做改變所需要的費用。

瓦勒斯：呃，如果我們決定放棄懲罰費用，把出貨日期往後延兩個禮拜呢？

總裁： 當然好，那對優博科技而言行得通。但是我們會卡在他們的貨上。

露西： 如果說我們放棄 50% 的罰款，將費用攤入他們的下一筆訂單，從長遠來看我們就不會有任何損失，也能留住一個好客戶。

瓦勒斯：我們也讓他們知道我們願意盡我們所能來滿足他們的需求。

總裁： 呃，你們兩個真的認為優博科技就長遠來看會是個好客戶？

瓦勒斯：當然，我已經和洛藍發展良好的關係。我們就把罰款減半，然後把這筆加到他們以後的合約裡。我覺得這是個雙贏的解決辦法，而且我想我可以說服洛藍接受。

Word List

conference call [ˋkɑnfərəns ˏkɔl] *n.* 電話會議（三方或以上利用電話進行通話討論）
cover [ˋkʌvɚ] *v.* 包含；覆蓋
be stuck V-ing 卡在……；困於……
write sth. into sth. 將某事物包含入另一事物中
in the long term 以長遠來看
win-win [ˋwɪnˋwɪn] *adj.* 雙贏的；雙方都獲利的
sell sth. to sb. 使某人接受某事物

3 Biz 加分句型 Nice-to-Know Phrases

CD II-11

3.1 開出你最後的價碼 Presenting Your Final Offer

談判時必須非常清楚自己的底線在哪，分寸一亂可能全盤盡輸。

❶ Well, the best I can do is ...
呃，我能做的最多就是……。

例 Well, the best I can do is to waive 50% of the penalty fee.
呃，我能做的最多就是放棄 50% 的懲罰費用。

❷ I can't move any further than ...
我無法做出比……更多的讓步。

例 I can't move any further than offering a 20% discount.
我無法做出比八折更多的讓步。

❸ I'm sorry. The best deal I can offer you is ...
對不起，我能給你們的最好條件是……。

例 I'm sorry. The best deal I can offer you is 15% off and no interest on the outstanding balance for six months.
對不起，我能給你們的最好條件是八五折和六個月未付餘額免利息。

❹ I wish I could do more, but ... is the best I can do.
我希望我還能做更多，但是……是我能做的極限。

例 I wish I could do more, but 25% off is the best I can do.
我希望我還能做更多，但是七五折是我能做的極限。

Word List

present [prɪ`zɛnt] *v.* 提出；呈現
offer [`ɔfɚ] *n./v.* 提供；出價
discount [`dɪskaʊnt] *n.* 折扣；*v.* 打折
15% off 去除 15%，即打 85 折
interest [`ɪntərɪst] *n.*（不可數）利息
outstanding [ˌaʊt`stændɪŋ] *adj.* 未償付的；未解決的
balance [`bæləns] *n.* 餘款；結存；剩餘部分

3.2 轉移責任 Shifting Responsibility

適時地搬出某人來共同承擔責任是一種聰明的做法；一來表示你已經盡所能爲對方爭取最大利益，二來對方若怪罪起來也不好意思將氣全出在你身上。

❶ I've spoken to (name/position) and he/she says that we can/can't ...（搬出主管或其他重要決策者）

我已經和（姓名／職稱）說過了，他／她說我們可以／不能……。

例 I've spoken to my manager and he says that we can't reduce the shipping costs.

我已經和我的經理說過了，他說我們不能減少運費。

❷ I spoke to both (person/department) and (person/department) and they both said that ...（以雙重阻力表示難度）

我跟（某人／部門）和（某人／部門）都談過了，他們都說……。

例 I spoke to both shipping and the production and they both said that we can't change the shipment date.

我跟出貨部門和生產部門都談過了，他們都說我們不能更改出貨日期。

❸ Our (position) says that any changes to ... are impossible.（表示沒有變更的餘地）

我們（職稱）說任何……的更改都是不可能的。

例 Our accountant says that any changes to payment dates are impossible.

我們會計說付款日期做任何改變都是不可能的。

❹ Let me talk to (name/position) to see if we can do anything for you.（不想或無法斷然拒絕時）

讓我和（姓名／職稱）談談，看我們是不是能幫你（們）做什麼。

例 Let me talk to our executive vice president to see if we can do anything for you.

讓我和執行副總談談，看我們是不是能幫你們做什麼。

shift [ʃɪft] *v.* 轉移；改變

accountant [ə`kauntənt] *n.* 會計人員

executive vice president [ɪg`zɛkjutɪv `vaɪs `prɛzədənt] *n.* 執行副總

小心陷阱

☹ 錯誤用法

I wish I **can** do more, but this is **my best to do**.

我希望我還能做更多，但這是我能做到的極限。

☺ 正確用法

I wish I **could** do more, but this is **the best I can do**.

我希望我還能做更多，但這是我能做到的極限。

文化小叮嚀

As an export country, Taiwan is likely to have more experience doing business with other cultures than the clients you are dealing with. You'll be surprised to know that most US business school graduates have not taken any courses in international business.

身為一個出口國，台灣很可能比正與你進行交易的客戶擁有更多與其他文化通商的經驗。你將訝於知道大部分的美國商學院畢業生從未上過國貿課程。

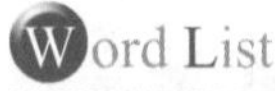

be likely to V. 很可能……

have experience doing sth. 有做某事的經驗

graduate [`grædʒuɪt] *n.* 畢業生

take a course 修課

4 實戰演練 Practice Exercises

I 請為下列三題選出最適本章的中文譯義。

❶ go over something

(A) 略過某事 (B) 檢視某事 (C) 考慮某事

❷ eat into

(A) 分攤 (B) 吃光 (C) 耗費

❸ be subject to ...

(A) 因為…… (B) 以……為條件 (C) 被……吸引

II 請根據你聽到的內容為下列兩題選出正確解答。

❶ What is Max willing to offer?

(A) A reduced shipping cost.

(B) An earlier delivery date.

(C) A discount on the price of the product.

❷ What does Kim want?

(A) A 20% reduction in shipping costs.

(B) An earlier delivery date.

(C) A 10% reduction in shipping costs and the original delivery date.

III 你和你的主管討論過了，關於這次的 case ，運費七五折是你們最大的讓步。在處理公司發生的實際狀況前，利用下列詞語寫一篇短文模擬一下情境，訓練一下自己的談判技巧吧。

discuss	alternatives to	accommodate
what if	work	the best we can
by 25%		

＊解答請見 236 頁

計劃電訪
Planning a Call

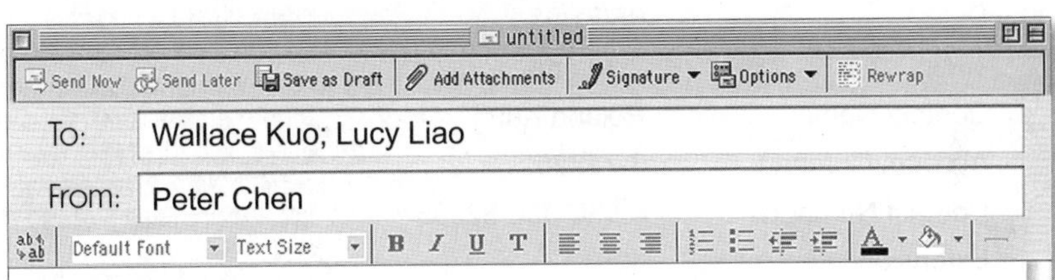

Please try and maintain better call records. I know that you already keep call records, but we need to standardize our records and use a format we can all understand easily.

Thanks,
Peter

請試著維護更佳的電訪記錄。我知道你們都已經有保存電訪記錄，但我們需要將我們的記錄標準化，並使用一種我們大家都容易懂的格式。

謝謝，
彼得

1 Master Call Plan

This section includes the key information about the company and your contact.

Company:	Ubertech
Date:	05/21/05
Time:	2:30 pm
Contact Name:	Roland Kuhn
Account Number:	3-74328
Contact Number:	49-30-838-52295
Extension:	325
Time Zone:	UTC + 0100
Products:	Computer Peripherals (card readers, memory sticks)

- master plan [ˋmæstɚ ˏplæn] *n.* 計劃表；行動藍圖；總體規劃
- UTC 世界標準時間；世界協調時（Universal Time, Coordinated 的縮寫，取代舊制 GMT 格林威治標準時 Greenwich Mean Time，為目前世界使用的標準時間尺度，以原子鐘計時，較精準，台灣的國家標準時間為 UTC +8）
- peripheral [pəˋrɪfərəl] *n.*【電腦】周邊設備

Last Call

This section includes the key information you'll need for the call you are going to make.

Last Call Date:	05/15/05
Personal Information:	Roland is a football fan. Favorite team is United. Check Internet to see how his team is doing. (Contact's information)
Key Points:	Order for memory sticks and card readers finalized. (Decisions from last call)
Action Items:	None (Actions from last call)

電訪計劃表

這一部份包含客戶公司和你的聯絡人的基本資料。

公司：	優博科技
日期：	05/21/05
時間：	2:30 pm
聯絡人姓名：	洛藍・昆
客戶編號：	3-74328
聯絡電話：	49-30-838-52295
分機：	325
時區：	世界標準時間 + 1 小時
產品：	電腦周邊 （讀卡機、記憶卡）

上次通話

這一部份包含你將打的電話所需要的基本資料。

上次通話日期：	05/15/05
個人資料：	洛藍是個足球迷，最喜歡的球隊是聯合隊。查一下網路看他那一隊表現如何。（聯絡人的資料）
要項：	記憶卡和讀卡機的訂單已定案 （上次通話的決定）
行動項目：	無（上次通話的行動）

Current Call

This section includes the key information of what you are going to discuss.

Call Goals: Introduce next generation of card readers.

Vocabulary: Features, speed, versatile, next evolution

Useful sentence patterns:
How have sales been lately?
How is the market in Germany?
I'm calling to talk with you about the next generation of our card reader.
Business has been fabulous.
(Sentence patterns you will use)

Call Decisions

In this section, you record the details from the call. Some of this information will become the Background Information for the next call.

Discussion Details:
No sale.
Ubertech is moving away from card readers.
Sales have been sluggish.
Economy is weak!
Spoke about United (football).

Action Items: None

本次電訪

這個部分包含你要討論的基本資料。

- generation [ˌdʒɛnəˋreʃən] *n.* 一代的人或事物；世代
- versatile [ˋvɝsətl] *adj.*（器物）多功能的；（人）多才多藝的
- evolution [ˌɛvəˋluʃən] *n.* 進化；發展
- fabulous [ˋfæbjələs] *adj.* 很讚的；極好的
- move away from N. 不再持有（某想法、習慣）、使用（某方式）；脫離……
- sluggish [ˋslʌgɪʃ] *adj.* 遲緩的；蕭條的

電訪目標： 介紹新一代的讀卡機。
字彙： 特性、速度、多功能的、新進化
實用句型： 最近銷量如何？
德國的市場如何？
我打來跟你聊一下我們新一代的讀卡機。
生意一直都非常好。
（你將使用的句型）

電訪決議

你在這個部分記錄電訪詳情。這些資料的某部份將成為下次電訪的背景資訊。

討論細節： 沒有業績。
優博科技正逐漸抽離讀卡機市場。
銷量一直動得很慢。
經濟疲弱！
談了聯合隊（足球）。
行動項目： 無

2 實戰會話 Show Time

CD II-13

14.1 Dialogue

Wallace calls Roland to introduce the next generation of card readers.

Wallace: Hello, Roland. How are you?

Roland: I'm fine. How are you doing, Wallace?

Wallace: Great! Things are really good. I was watching CNN last night. I see that United is on <u>a winning streak</u>.

Roland: They are having their best season in years.

Wallace: How has the market in Germany been?

Roland: Not so good. The economy is weak and sales have been sluggish. How is the market on your end?

Wallace: It's been great. I have no complaints.

Roland: I'm glad to hear that. What can I do for you today, Wallace?

Wallace: I'm calling to talk with you about the next generation of our card readers.

Roland: I'm sure they are great, Wallace, but I have to tell you that we are moving away from card readers.

譯文

瓦勒斯打電話給洛藍介紹新一代的讀卡機。

瓦勒斯：哈囉，洛藍。你好嗎？

洛藍：　我很好。你好嗎，瓦勒斯？

瓦勒斯：很不錯！一切都很好。我昨晚看 CNN ，我知道聯合隊目前連勝。

洛藍：　這是幾年來他們最好的一季。

瓦勒斯：德國的市場近來怎麼樣？

洛藍：　不是很好。經濟很差，銷量動得很慢。你那邊的市場怎樣？

瓦勒斯：一直都不錯。我沒啥怨言。

洛藍：　很高興聽到你這麼說。今天我能幫你什麼忙，瓦勒斯？

瓦勒斯：我打電話來跟你聊一下我們新一代的讀卡機。

洛藍：　我相信它們一定很棒，瓦勒斯，但我必須告訴你我們正逐漸抽離讀卡機市場。

a winning streak 連勝（streak [strik] *n.* 條紋）

3 電訪計劃模板 Templates for the Master Call Plan

這個單元我們提供了兩組表單模板，包括電訪計劃表、上次通話、本次電訪及電訪決議，讓你用來維護你和客戶的通話記錄。

Master Call Plan

Company:

Date:

Time:

Contact Name:

Account Number:

Contact Number:

Extension:

Time Zone:

Products:

Last Call

Last Call Date:

Personal Information:

Key Points:

Action Items:

Current Call

Call Goals:

Vocabulary:

Useful sentence patterns:

Call Decisions

Discussion Details:

Action Items:

電訪計劃表

公司：

日期：

時間：

聯絡人姓名：

客戶編號：

聯絡電話：

分機：

時區：

產品：

上次通話

上次通話日期：

個人資料：

要項：

行動項目：

本次電訪

電訪目標：

字彙：

實用句型：

電訪決議

討論細節：

行動項目：

小心陷阱

☹ 錯誤用法

The weather **is** great lately and I **have always playing** some golf.

最近天氣都很好，我一直有在打些高爾夫球。

☺ 正確用法

The weather **has been** great lately and I'**ve been playing** some golf.

最近天氣都很好，我一直有在打些高爾夫球。

文化小叮嚀

As in many Asian nations, numbers are very important to Italians. If you are invited to a business associate's home, it is customary to take chocolates, pastries, wine (only very good wine) or flowers. However, never take an even (2,4,8,10 etc.) number of flowers (except for 1/2 dozen and 1 dozen). Additionally, most Italians have two business cards, one for business, and another for less formal relationships.

就像在很多亞洲國家，數字對義大利人也非常重要。如果你受邀到一個生意夥伴的家裡，習慣是要帶些巧克力、糕餅、酒（只能帶很好的酒）或花；但是，千萬不可以帶一束偶數（2, 4, 8, 10 等）的花（半打和一打除外）。此外，大部分的義大利人擁有兩張名片，一張做生意時用，另一張則針對比較非正式的關係使用。

Word List

associate [ə`soʃɪɪt] *n.* 同事；夥伴

customary [`kʌstəm,ɛrɪ] *adj.* 習慣的；按慣例的

pastry [`pestrɪ] *n.* 糕餅；酥皮點心

even [`ivən] *adj.* 偶數的；平均的

except for ... 除了……之外

dozen [`dʌzn̩] *n.* 一打； 12 個

additionally [ə`dɪʃənl̩ɪ] *adv.* 此外；附加地

實戰演練 Practice Exercises

I 請為下列兩題選出最適本章的中文譯義。

❶ move away from ...

(A) 搬離…… (B) 戒掉…… (C) 抽離……

❷ be on a winning streak

(A) 具冠軍相 (B) 連勝中 (C) 全勝

II 請根據你聽到的內容為下列兩題選出正確解答。

CD II-14

❶ Why can't the delivery be made on Monday?

(A) It's a little too rushed.

(B) The post office is closed on Mondays.

(C) Monday is a holiday.

❷ When will Rhoda send the man the tracking number?

(A) On Monday morning.

(B) After the shipment is sent out.

(C) On Tuesday.

III 你要打電話向客戶介紹兩樣產品的進化版。好口才多半不是與生俱來的，所以平時就該找機會訓練訓練。利用下列詞語寫一篇短文練習一下吧。

want to talk	next evolution/generation of	sales
move away from	have great success with	hear about

＊解答請見 238 頁

留言
Leaving a Message

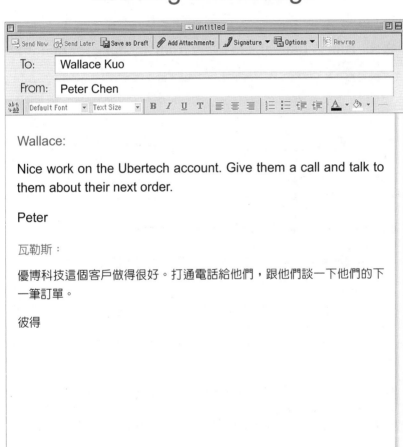

untitled

Send Now | Send Later | Save as Draft | Add Attachments | Signature | Options | Rewrap

To: Wallace Kuo

From: Peter Chen

Default Font | Text Size

Wallace:

Nice work on the Ubertech account. Give them a call and talk to them about their next order.

Peter

瓦勒斯：

優博科技這個客戶做得很好。打通電話給他們，跟他們談一下他們的下一筆訂單。

彼得

1 Biz 必通句型 Need-to-Know Phrases

1.1 編錄個人訊息 Programming Your Message

下列八句教你編錄個人語音信箱，讓來電者知道你現在不方便或無法接聽電話。先從表示身分讓來電者知道信箱主人是誰開始，再說明無法接聽電話的原因。

❶ Hi. This is (name). I'm away from my desk for (length of time).
嗨，我是（姓名）。我（時間長度）都不會在位子上。

例 Hi. This is Roland. I'm away from my desk for the rest of the day.
嗨，我是洛藍。我接下來整天都不會在位子上。

❷ This is (name). I can't make it to the phone (when).
我是（姓名）。我（何時）無法接聽電話。

例 This is Wallace Kuo. I can't make it to the phone right now.
我是瓦勒斯・郭。我現在無法接聽電話。

❸ This is (name). I won't be able to take/return your call until....
我是（姓名）。我在⋯⋯之前都無法接聽／回您的電話。

例 This is Timothy Chao. I'm out of the office, and I won't be able to return your call until next week.
我是提莫西・趙。我現在不在辦公室，我在下星期之前都無法回您的電話。

接著，請對方留下訊息及聯絡資料；前者幫助你判斷事情緩急，後者讓你順利回覆。

❹ Please specify the reason for your call and your ...
請詳細說明您來電的原因及您的⋯⋯。

例 Please specify the reason for you call and your contact information.
請詳細說明您來電的原因及您的聯絡資料。

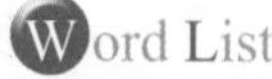

Word List

program [ˋprogræm] *v.* 編排；計劃；使⋯⋯按照預定步驟表現工作

make it somewhere 順利到達某處

specify [ˋspɛsə͵faɪ] *v.* 詳細指明；清楚解說

❺ Please leave a detailed message, including ...

請留下詳細的訊息，包括……。

例 Please leave a detailed message, including your name, number and time of call.

請留下詳細的訊息，包括您的名字、電話號碼及來電時間。

最後，告訴對方你什麼時候可能回電，讓留言者有個預期；此外，別忘了「嗶一聲之後請留言」這樣貼心的指示。

❻ I will call you back (when). Please leave a message after ...

我會在（何時）回電給您。請在……之後留言。

例 I will call you back within 24 hours. Please leave a message after the tone.

我會在 24 小時之內回電給您。請在提示音之後留言。

❼ I'll be back in (place) on (date). Please leave a message after you ...

我會在（日期）回到（地點）。請您在……之後留言。

例 I'll be back in the office on Tuesday. Please leave a message after you hear the beep.

我會在星期二回到辦公室。請您在聽到嗶聲之後留言。

❽ I will return your call (when). Please leave a message when you hear the beep/tone.

我會（何時）回您的電話。請您在聽到嗶聲／提示音後留言。

例 I will return your call as soon as I get a chance. Please leave a message when you hear the tone.

我一有機會就會回您的電話。請您在聽到提示音後留言。

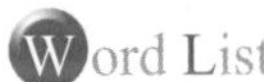

detailed [`diteld] *adj.* 詳細的

tone [ton] *n.* 音；音調；聲調

beep [bip] *n./v.*（發出）嗶嗶聲

1.2 留言 Leaving a Message

下列八句讓你學會如何簡單扼要地留下一通語音訊息。同樣也是從表明身分開始，並記錄留言的時刻、日期，以幫助聽者判斷留言時間點。

❶ This is (name) from (company). It's (time/date).

我是（公司）的（姓名）。現在／今天是（時間／日期）。

例 This is Marie from Omega Electronics. It's Tuesday, May 23.

我是歐美嘉電子的瑪莉。今天是五月二十三號，星期二。

❷ It's (name) calling from (company) at/on (time/date).

我是（姓名），（時間／日期）從（公司）打過來。

例 It's Hans Greenman calling from Fast Systems at 3:15.

我是漢斯・格林門，三點十五分從飛速特系統打過來。

❸ I'm calling to talk to you about ...

我打電話來跟您談……。

例 I'm calling to talk to you about a new order.

我打電話來跟您談一筆新訂單。

下列兩句用來說明聯絡事項。

❹ I need to discuss ... with you.

我需要和您討論……。

例 I need to discuss the price with you.

我需要和您討論價錢。

❺ I was hoping we could discuss ...

我原本希望我們能討論……。

例 I was hoping we could discuss our new products.

我原本希望我們能討論我們的新產品。

最後，讓對方知道你希望何時獲得回覆，千萬別忘了留下自己的聯絡方式。

6 Can you call me back (when)? You can reach me at (number).
您能（何時）回電給我嗎？您打（電話號碼）就可以找到我。

例 Can you call me back as soon as you get a chance? You can reach me at 886-2-2371-8989.
您能不能一有機會就回電給我？您打 886-2-2371-8989 就可以找到我。

7 Is it possible you could get back to me (when)? My number is ...
您有沒有可能（何時）回電給我？我的號碼是……。

例 Is it possible you could get back to me sometime tomorrow? My number is 1-415-828-4538.
您有沒有可能明天哪個時候回電給我？我的號碼是 1-415-828-4538 。

8 I'm hoping we can talk about ... no later than (when). My number is ...
我希望我們最晚不超過（何時）談……。我的號碼是……。

例 I'm hoping we can talk about your new order no later than next Monday. My number is 44-20-7771-2345.
我希望最晚不超過下星期一可以跟您談一下您的新訂單。我的號碼是 44-20-7771-2345 。

reach [ritʃ] *v.* 與……取得聯繫；伸手靠近；抵達

2 實戰會話 Show Time

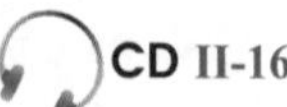
CD II-16

2.1 Dialogue

Wallace Kuo calls Roland Kuhn to talk about Ubertech's new order. Unfortunately, Roland is out of the office.

Wallace: Hello. Can I speak to Roland Kuhn, please?

Receptionist: I'll put you through to Mr. Kuhn. Please hold.

Roland's voice mail: This is Roland. I'm away from my desk for the rest of the day. Please leave a detailed message, including your name, number and time of call. I will call you back within 24 hours. Please start your message when you hear the beep.

Wallace tries to call Roland back the next day.

Wallace: Hello. Is Roland Kuhn in?

Receptionist: Let me transfer you to Mr. Kuhn's office. Please hold.

Wallace: Thank you.

Roland's voice mail: This is Roland. I can't make it to the phone right now. Please specify the reason for your call and your contact information. Please leave a message after you hear the tone.

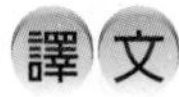

瓦勒斯．郭打電話給洛藍．昆談優博科技的新訂單。不巧的是洛藍不在辦公室。

瓦勒斯：　　　喂。我可以跟洛藍．昆講話嗎，麻煩你？

總機：　　　　我幫您轉接昆先生。請稍等。

洛藍的語音信箱：我是洛藍，我接下來整天都不會在位子上。請留下詳細的訊息，包括您的名字、電話號碼及來電時間。我會在二十四小時以內回電給您。請您在聽到嗶聲後開始留言。

隔天瓦勒斯試著再打電話給洛藍。

瓦勒斯：　　　喂。洛藍．昆在嗎？

總機：　　　　我幫您轉到昆先生的辦公室。請稍等。

瓦勒斯：　　　謝謝。

洛藍的語音信箱：我是洛藍。我現在無法接聽電話。請詳細說明您來電的原因及您的聯絡資料。請您在聽到提示音之後留言。

voice mail [ˋvɔɪs͵mel] *n.* 語音信箱 (= voicemail)

2.2 Dialogue

Lucy is calling Marie to talk to her about some new products Omega is developing. She needs to ensure that she covers all the bases in a short message.

(Scenario 1)

Marie: Hi. This is Marie. I'm away from my desk for the rest of the day. Please leave a detailed message, including your name, number and time of call. I will call you back within 24 hours. Please leave a message when you hear the beep.

Lucy: This is Lucy from Omega Electronics. It's Tuesday, May 23. I am hoping we can find a time to discuss our new products. Can you call me back as soon as you get a chance? You can reach me at 886-2-2371-8989.

(Scenario 2)

Marie: Hi, This is Marie. I'm away from my desk for the rest of the day. Please leave a detailed message, including your name, number and time of call. I will call you back within 24 hours. Please leave a message when you hear the beep.

Lucy: It's Lucy calling from Omega Electronics at 4:28 in the afternoon. I need to discuss the new order with you. I'm hoping we can talk about it as soon as you get back. My number is 886-2-2371-8989. I'll be waiting for your call.

譯文

露西正打電話給瑪莉，要告訴她一些關於歐美嘉正在研發的新產品。她必須確定她在簡短的訊息裡包含所有的重要事項。

（場景 1）

瑪莉：嗨，我是瑪莉。我接下來整天都不會在位子上。請留下詳細的訊息，包括您的名字、電話號碼及來電時間。我會在二十四小時之內回電給您。請您在聽到嗶聲後留言。

露西：我是歐美嘉電子的露西。今天是五月二十三號，星期二。我希望我們能找個時間討論一下我們的新產品。妳能不能一有機會就回電給我？妳打 886-2-2371-8989 就可以找到我。

（場景 2）

瑪莉：嗨，我是瑪莉。我接下來整天都不會在位子上。請留下詳細的訊息，包括您的名字、電話號碼及來電時間。我會在二十四小時之內回電給您。請您在聽到嗶聲後留言。

露西：我是露西，下午四點二十八分從歐美嘉電子打過來。我需要和妳討論那份新訂單。我希望等妳一回來我們就能談談。我的號碼是 886-2-2371-8989 ，我會等妳的電話。

3 Biz 加分句型 Nice-to-Know Phrases

CD II-17

3.1 當你無法完整留完你的訊息時 You Are Unable to Complete Your Message

造成留言中斷的原因有很多，有可能是容許留言的時間太短，也可能是說到一半被打斷。

❶ **This is part two of the message left by (name).**（表明留言承接上通）
這是（姓名）留言的第二部分。

例 This is part two of the message left by David.
這是大衛留言的第二部分。

❷ **I'm sorry ... This is (name) calling back.**（說明分段的原因）
對不起……。我是（姓名）再打過來的。

例 I'm sorry. I got cut off. This is Tania calling back.
對不起。我剛被切斷。我是坦妮雅再打過來的。

當然也可能是因爲有後續發展而必須補充、更正，或者只是忘記說。

❸ **This is (name) again. I wanted to add ...**
又是我，（姓名）。我想補充……。

例 This is Hans again. I wanted to add that I won't be in the office tomorrow.
又是我，漢斯。我想補充我明天不會在辦公室。

❹ **It's (name) again. I forgot to mention ...**
又是我，（姓名）。我忘記說……。

例 It's Marie again. I forgot to mention that I'll attend a meeting tomorrow morning, so it's better if you call back in the afternoon.
又是我，瑪莉。我忘記說我明天早上會參加一個會議，所以你下午回電會比較好。

Word List

cut off *phr. v.* 切斷；中斷

3.2 你可能留錯信箱 You Might Have the Wrong Machine

打電話會撥錯號碼，留言也可能會留錯信箱；有此疑慮時，可用下列三句表明。

❶ I'm not sure that I have the right person. I'm calling for (name).
我不確定我是不是打對人。我打電話要找的是（姓名）。

例 I'm not sure that I have the right person. I'm calling for Johnson Whitman.
我不確定我是不是打對人。我打電話要找的是強森．惠特曼。

❷ Is this (name)'s (voicemail/machine)? I'm calling to talk about ...
這是（姓名）的語音信箱嗎？我打來談……。

例 Is this Cynthia's voicemail? I'm calling to talk about a new order.
這是欣希雅的語音信箱嗎？我打來談一筆新訂單。

❸ I hope this is (name)'s (voicemail/machine). I wanted to talk to you about ...
我希望這是（姓名）的語音信箱。我想跟您談……。

例 I hope this is Sylvia's machine. I wanted to talk to you about a new product.
我希望這是絲薇亞的語音信箱。我想跟妳談一個新產品。

如果你留的是系統語音信箱，下列這句有助聽取留言者快速分類，儘早安排相關人員回覆你的需求。

❹ I'm looking for someone who can help me with ...
我在找能幫我……的人。

例 I'm looking for someone who can help me with a few questions I have about your services.
我對你們的服務有一些問題，我在找能夠幫我解答這些問題的人。

小心陷阱

☹ 錯誤用法

I can't **make to** the phone right now. Please **leave message** after you hear **bee**.

我現在無法接聽電話。聽您在聽到嗶聲之後留言。

☺ 正確用法

I can't **make it to** the phone right now. Please **leave a message** after you hear **the beep**.

我現在無法接聽電話。請您在聽到嗶聲之後留言。

文化小叮嚀

The latest trend in outsourcing means that you might end up speaking with a person in India when you call companies such as Daimler-Chrysler, British Telecom, Barclays Bank, HSBC, or Dell. There are as many as 200,000 employees working at call centers in India. Market reports say the industry could generate US$1.7 billion by 2008.

最新的委外趨勢意味當你打電話給像戴姆勒克萊斯勒、英國電訊、巴克萊銀行、匯豐銀行或戴爾電腦等公司時，最後可能是跟在印度的人講話。印度有高達二十萬的雇員在電話客服中心工作。市場報告指出，這個產業到了 2008 年能夠產出 17 億美金。

Word List

outsourcing [ˋaut͵sɔrsɪŋ] *n.* 委外（將公司組織內的活動發外包由外部人員製作）

end up Ving 最後處於做……的情況；以做……爲結尾

Barclays Bank [ˋbɑr͵klɪz ˋbæŋk] *n.* 英商巴克萊銀行（總部在倫敦）

call center [ˋkɔl ͵sɛntɚ] *n.* 電話客服中心（公司機構接應客戶來電及作電話行銷拜訪的作業單位，業務亦常包括電子郵件、傳眞及書信等）

industry [ˋɪndəstrɪ] *n.* 產業；工業

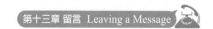

4 實戰演練 Practice Exercises

I 請為下列三題選出最適本章的中文譯義。

❶ can't make it to the phone

(A) 來不及接電話 (B) 接不到電話 (C) 無法接聽電話

❷ get cut off

(A) 被切斷 (B) 被干擾 (C) 被阻礙

❸ forget to mention ...

(A) 忘記曾說過…… (B) 忘記說…… (C) 放棄說……

II 請根據你聽到的內容為下列兩題選出正確解答。

❶ What is Pamela's relationship to Daniel?

(A) She is a potential customer.

(B) She is a potential supplier.

(C) She is a potential employee.

❷ When does Pamela want to pay for the goods?

(A) When they are delivered.

(B) 30 days after they are delivered.

(C) 60 days after they are delivered.

III 你打了幾通電話給客戶，但運氣不好，都沒人接而直接轉進語音系統，為了顧及辦公效率，你決定留言。沒人接聽的情況你一定遇過，但轉進語音信箱時你是否會選擇留言？利用下列詞語寫一篇短文練習一下，好好地利用這項便利的科技吧。

this is/it's	call from	at/in/on
hope/need to	discuss/talk about	get back to
my number		

＊解答請見 240 頁

打電話開發
Cold Calling

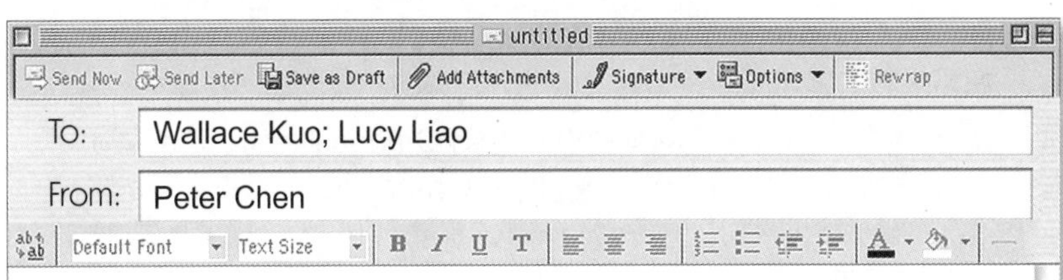

We need to unload 10,000 64MB memory sticks. Knock 20% off the price and see if we can get some new customers interested.

Good luck,
Peter

我們需要脫手 10,000 張 64MB 的記憶卡。減少 20% 的價錢，看我們是不是能找到有興趣的買主。

祝好運，
彼得

1 Biz 必通句型 Need-to-Know Phrases

1.1 開場白 Introduction

開發是推廣業務非常重要的一項工作，而電話是開發常用的一種工具；用下列兩句簡單地介紹一下自己和公司的產業性質。

❶ Hi. My name is ... from (company). We <u>specialize in</u> ...
您好，我的名字叫……，從（公司）打來的。我們專門生產……。

例 Hi. My name is Wallace Kuo from Omega Electronics. We specialize in computer <u>peripheral</u> products.
您好，我的名字叫瓦勒斯・郭，從歐美嘉電子打來的。我們專門生產電腦周邊商品。

❷ Hello, my name is ... I'm with (company). We are a leader in ...
您好，我的名字叫……。我在（公司）工作。我們是……的領導品牌。

例 Hello, my name is Lucy Liao. I'm with Omega Electronics. We are a leader in computer <u>accessories</u> and peripherals.
您好，我的名字叫露西・廖。我在歐美嘉電子工作。我們是電腦配件和周邊設備的領導品牌。

幽默常造成加分效果，並容易讓人留下深刻的印象；下列兩句是比較俏皮的開場方式。

❸ I'm sure you get a lot of <u>cold calls</u>. Well, ...
我相信您一定常接到許多推銷電話。呃，……。

例 I'm sure you get a lot of cold calls. Well, <u>strap yourself in</u>. Here's another.
我相信您一定常接到許多推銷電話。呃，準備好，這是另外一通。

Word List

specialize [`spɛʃəl͵aɪz] *v.* 專門從事；專攻 (+ in sth.)
peripheral [pə`rɪfərəl] *n.*【電腦】周邊設備
accessory [æk`sɛsərɪ] *n.* 配件；附件
cold call [`kold `kɔl] *n.* 推銷電話／ *v.* 打電話開發
strap oneself in 繫上安全帶準備上路

❹ You guessed it. It's a cold call, but ...
您猜對了。這是通推銷電話，但……。

例 You guessed it. It's a cold call, but I'll keep it <u>short and very sweet</u>.
您猜對了。這是通推銷電話，但是我會盡量讓它簡短悅耳。

下列四句是比較禮貌的說法，以詢問的方式試探對方。

❺ Do you have a few minutes to talk about ...?
您有沒有幾分鐘的時間聊聊……？

例 Do you have a few minutes to talk about increasing your sales?
您有沒有幾分鐘的時間聊聊如何增加你們的銷售額？

❻ Can I take a few minutes to ask you about ...?
我能不能利用幾分鐘的時間請問您……？

例 Can I take a few minutes to ask you about your business?
我能不能利用幾分鐘的時間請問您你們的營業狀況？

❼ I'd like to talk to you about ... Do you have a few minutes?
我想跟您談談……。您有幾分鐘的時間嗎？

例 I'd like to talk to you about how Omega Electronics can improve your business. Do you have a few minutes?
我想跟您談談歐美嘉電子能如何改善你們的業績。您有幾分鐘的時間嗎？

❽ Are you busy right now, or is there a better time to ...?
您現在正在忙嗎？或者有沒有更適當的時間……？

例 Are you busy right now, or is there a better time to introduce our products?
您現在正在忙嗎？或者有沒有更適當的時間可以介紹我們的產品？

short and sweet 簡單易懂且切題；簡短好聽

1.2 推銷話術 The Pitch

說話是學問，而且是門相當高深的學問，如何讓聽者動心、怨者平息、怒者滿意，端賴你的技巧與方式；其中，誠意及自信是必需的態度。

❶ I want to tell you about ...

我想告訴您關於……。

例 I want to tell you about a fabulous new product that our customers have had great success with.

我想告訴您關於一個讓我們客戶都獲得成功經驗的優質新產品。

❷ If you are looking for ..., then I've got the right ... for you.

如果您正在尋找……，那我正好有適合您的……。

例 If you are looking for a product that flies off the shelves, then I've got the right product for you.

如果您正在尋找一個能夠大賣的商品，那我正好有適合您的產品。

❸ I have (adj), (adj) (product) that are ..., which I can ...

我有（形容詞）、（形容詞）而且……的（產品），我能……。

例 I have new, mini memory sticks that are pulling customers into stores, which I can offer at the lowest price in the market.

我有新穎、迷你而且能吸引顧客自動上門的記憶卡，我能以市面最低價提供。

❹ We are introducing a (adj.), (adj), (adj) (product) that can ...

我們正推出一款（形容詞）、（形容詞）、（形容詞）而且能……的（產品）。

例 We are introducing a sleek, new, mini memory stick that can be tailored to you needs.

我們正推出一款時髦、新穎、迷你而且能依您的需求訂做的記憶卡。

pitch [pɪtʃ] *n.* 推銷話語／ *v.* 推銷

(sth.) flies off the shelf/shelves（某物）賣得很好

sleek [slik] *adj.* 時尚的；雅緻的

be tailored to ... 依……被訂製

❺ I'd like to introduce ...

我想介紹……。

例 I'd like to introduce a fantastic, new, mini memory stick.

我想介紹一款夢幻、新穎又迷你的記憶卡。

❻ We have (adj), (adj), (adj.) (product) that ...

我們有（形容詞）、（形容詞）又（形容詞），而且……的（產品）。

例 We have fantastic, new, mini memory sticks that can be branded with your logo and color at no extra cost.

我們有夢幻、新穎又迷你，而且能讓你們打上你們的商標和顏色，不需支付額外費用的記憶卡。

❼ We are offering a special discount of (amount) to our new customers for ...

我們現在正提供（數量）的特別折扣給我們……新客戶。

例 We are offering a special discount of 20% to our new customers for our memory sticks.

我們現在正提供 20% 的特別折扣給我們記憶卡新客戶。

❽ I/We have ... that ...

我／我們有……而且……。

例 I have new, mini memory sticks that are selling themselves.

我有新穎、迷你而且大受歡迎、銷路很好的記憶卡。

fantastic [fæn`tæstɪk] *adj.* 夢幻的；驚人的

brand [brænd] *v.* 打印商標

(sth.) sells itself（某物）本身受歡迎、賣得好

2 實戰會話 Show Time

2.1 Dialogue

Wallace Kuo calls a company in France to try and generate some new business.

2.1a

Wallace: Hi. My name is Wallace Kuo from Omega Electronics. We specialize in computer peripheral products.

Francois: Well ..., what can I do for you?

Wallace: You guessed it. It's a cold call, but I will keep it short and very sweet. I have new, mini memory sticks that are pulling customers into stores, which I can offer at the lowest price in the market. Are you interested?

2.1b

Wallace: Hi. My name is Wallace Kuo. I'm with Omega Electronics. We are a leader in computer accessories and peripherals. I'm sure you get a lot of cold calls. Well, strap yourself in. Here's another. I'd like to talk to you about how Omega Electronics can improve your business. Do you have a few minutes?

Francois: I'm a little busy right now.

Wallace: Is there a better time to call you back?

Francois: Tomorrow would be fine.

Wallace: What time would be good for you?

Francois: Two o'clock in the afternoon.

Wallace: Great, talk to you then.

譯文

瓦勒斯・郭 打電話給一家在法國的公司，嘗試創造一些新生意。

會話 2.1a

瓦勒斯： 您好，我的名字叫瓦勒斯・郭，從歐美嘉電子打來的。我們專門生產電腦周邊商品。

法蘭斯沃：呃……，我能為你做什麼？

瓦勒斯： 您猜對了。這是通推銷電話，但是我會盡量讓它簡短悅耳。我有新穎、迷你而且能吸引顧客自動上門的記憶卡，我能以市面最低價提供。您有興趣嗎？

會話 2.1b

瓦勒斯： 您好，我的名字叫瓦勒斯・郭。我在歐美嘉電子工作。我們是電腦配件與周邊設備的領導品牌。我相信您一定常接到許多推銷電話。呃，準備好，這是另外一通。我想和您談談歐美嘉電子能如何改善你們的業績。您有幾分鐘的時間嗎？

法蘭斯沃：我現在有點忙。

瓦勒斯： 有沒有更適當的時間回電給您？

法蘭斯沃：明天可以。

瓦勒斯： 您什麼時候比較方便？

法蘭斯沃：下午兩點。

瓦勒斯： 太好了，到時候再和您談。

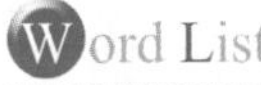

generate [ˋʤɛnəˏret] *v.* 產生；引起

2.2 Dialogue

Wallace now has to pitch the product. His goal is to make Francois interested.

2.2a A Good Start

Wallace: Let's continue our conversation. I want to tell you about a fabulous new product that our customers have had great success with.

Francois: Sure.

Wallace: I have new, mini memory sticks that are selling themselves.

Francois: I like it when products sell themselves. Tell me more about them.

2.2b Trouble Ahead

Wallace: If you are looking for a product that flies off the shelves, then I've got the right product for you.

Francois: Well, we are always looking for products with great turnover. What do you have?

Wallace: We have fantastic, new, mini memory sticks that can be branded with your logo and color at no extra cost.

Francois: We already have a line of memory sticks.

Wallace: Well, we are offering a special discount of 20% to our new customers for our memory sticks.

Francois: Tempting, but no thanks. Still, thanks for introducing them.

譯文

瓦勒斯現在必須推銷產品。他的目標是讓法蘭斯沃感興趣。

會話 2.2a ——好的開始

瓦勒斯：　我們繼續我們的對話吧。我想告訴您關於一個讓我們客戶都獲得成功經驗的優質新產品。

法蘭斯沃：好。

瓦勒斯：　我有新穎、迷你而且大受歡迎、銷路很好的記憶卡。

法蘭斯沃：我喜歡產品自動賣得動。告訴我更多吧。

會話 2.2b ——「錢」途困難

瓦勒斯：　如果您正在尋找一個能夠大賣的商品，那我正好有適合您的產品。

法蘭斯沃：嗯，我們一直都在找銷售亮眼的產品。你有什麼？

瓦勒斯：　我們有很棒的新型迷你記憶卡，而且能讓你們不需支付額外費用就打上商標和顏色。

法蘭斯沃：我們已經有一系列的記憶卡了。

瓦勒斯：　呃，我們現在正提供 20% 的特別折扣給我們記憶卡新客戶。

法蘭斯沃：很誘人，但是不用了。不過還是謝謝你的介紹。

Word List

turnover [ˋtɝn͵ovɚ] *n.*（一段期間內的）營業額；成交量
a line of sth. 一系列的東西；一排的東西；一行的東西
tempting [ˋtɛmptɪŋ] *adj.* 誘惑人的；吸引人的

3 Biz 加分句型 Nice-to-Know Phrases

CD II-21

3.1 客戶不感興趣時 Customer Doesn't Bite

再好的產品都可能乏人問津，再糟的產品也能賣得出去，這就是絕大多數企業每年編列高額預算在行銷活動上的原因。推動業務除了需要運氣，更需要耐心和毅力，當客戶對你的介紹不感興趣時，別灰心！用下列四句再加把勁。

❶ Would you mind if I faxed you ...?（當你覺得提供詳細資料有助客戶考慮時）

您介不介意我傳真……給您？

例 Would you mind if I faxed you a copy of our catalog?
您介不介意我傳真一份我們的型錄給您？

❷ Would it be all right if I sent you a sample ...?（你想讓樣品自己說話）

如果我寄一個……樣品給您可以嗎？

例 Would it be all right if I sent you a sample memory stick?
如果我寄一個記憶卡樣品給您可以嗎？

❸ Can I send you ... for ...?（客戶如果沒有拒絕，可主動附上資料加強說服）

我可以寄……的……給您嗎？

例 Can I send you product specifications and the price list for our memory sticks?
我可以寄我們記憶卡的產品規格和價目表給您嗎？

❹ Do you mind telling me a bit about ... you already have?（希望瞭解競爭產品時）

您介意告訴我一些有關您現有的……嗎？

例 Do you mind telling me a bit about the memory sticks you already have?
您介意告訴我一些有關您現有記憶卡的資料嗎？

bite [baɪt] *v.* 上當；上鉤
a copy of sth. 一份東西；一份某事物的副本
catalog [ˋkætə͵lɔg] *n.* 型錄；目錄
sample [ˋsæmpḷ] *n.* 樣品；試用品
mind V-ing 介意……

3.2 該公司已經有供應商時 The Company Already Has a Supplier

有固定配合供應商的公司大部分比較不容易改變合作對象，這是頗具難度的一關。在表露誠心、發揮毅力、彰顯產品特性、換個方式進行了之後，如果對方依舊不爲所動，應該懂得「適可而止」的道理。過一陣子再試吧！別讓你的恆心變成了「死纏爛打」。

❶ **Yes, but you haven't seen ... or ... yet.**（希望客戶能比較過再答覆）

是，但您還沒看過……或……。

例 Yes, but you haven't seen our memory sticks or prices yet.

是，但您還沒看過我們的記憶卡或價格。

❷ **I'm sure we can offer you ...**（突顯對自家產品的信心）

我確定我們能提供您……。

例 I'm sure we can offer you better memory sticks at a better price.

我確定我們能以更好的價格提供您更好的記憶卡。

❸ **Well, we have the best ... in the market.**（希望獲得機會競爭）

嗯，我們有市場最好的……。

例 Well, we have the best memory sticks in the market.

嗯，我們有市場最好的記憶卡。

❹ **Our ... can't be <u>compared with</u> other ... on the market.**（強調產品的優越）

我們的……不能拿來和市面上其他的……做比較。

例 Our memory sticks can't be compared with other memory sticks on the market.

我們的記憶卡不能拿來和市面上其他的記憶卡做比較。

compare A with B 拿 A 和 B 相比

小心陷阱

☹ 錯誤用法

I have new, mini memory **stick** that are pulling customers **into doors, that** I can **give with the lowest price of market**.

我有新穎、迷你而且能吸引顧客自動上門的記憶卡，我能以市面最低價提供。

☺ 正確用法

I have new, mini memory **sticks** that are pulling customers **into stores, which** I can **offer at the lowest price in the market**.

我有新穎、迷你而且能吸引顧客自動上門的記憶卡，我能以市面最低價提供。

文化小叮嚀

Many businesspeople in the Middle East prefer to have discussions about current events before entering negotiations. In this way, they feel that they can get a better understanding of who you are. In fact, in some countries, it is considered rude to immediately begin negotiations.

很多中東商人比較喜歡在展開協商前先談論時事，他們認為這樣能更加瞭解你這個人。事實上，在某些國家，直接展開協商被認為是無禮的。

Word List

the Middle East [ðə `mɪdl̩ `ist] *n.* 中東地區

prefer to V. 比較喜歡……

current events [`kɝənt ɪ`vɛnts] *n.*（複數形）時事

negotiations [nɪˌgoʃɪ`eʃənz] *n.*（常用複數）協商；談判

4 實戰演練 Practice Exercises

I 請為下列三題選出最適本章的中文譯義。

1. specialize in ...

   (A) 詳細說明…… (B) 專門生產…… (C) 專攻……

2. short and sweet

   (A) 口蜜腹劍 (B) 深入淺出 (C) 簡短悅耳

3. something flies off the shelves

   (A) 某物來自庫存 (B) 某物從架上飛出去 (C) 某物賣得很好

II 請根據你聽到的內容為下列兩題選出正確解答。

1. Why does the woman ask who the man is?

   (A) They have never talked before.

   (B) She can't remember who he is.

   (C) She has forgotten where he works.

2. What does the man's company sell?

   (A) LCD monitors.

   (B) Memory sticks.

   (C) Mice.

III 你今天的主要工作是開發，除了需要撰寫十封開發信外，兩天前上頭給了你一份名單要你主動打電話聯絡。同志，我們知道創業維艱、革命不易，拿起話筒前，利用下列詞語寫一篇短文模擬一下實境。記住！練習會讓你的表現更好。

my name is	cold call	a leader in
a few minutes	unload	in the market

＊解答請見 242 頁

操作電話語音系統 Navigating Phone Systems

untitled

Send Now | Send Later | Save as Draft | Add Attachments | Signature | Options | Rewrap

To: Wallace Kuo

From: Peter Chen

Default Font | Text Size

Wallace:

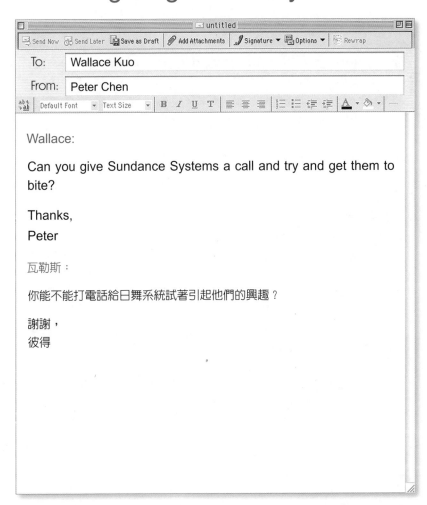

Can you give Sundance Systems a call and try and get them to bite?

Thanks,
Peter

瓦勒斯：

你能不能打電話給日舞系統試著引起他們的興趣？

謝謝，
彼得

1 Biz 必通句型 Need-to-Know Phrases

商務電訪一定會遇到打電話進入語音系統的情況，本單元列舉 16 句語音系統的基本常見指令，為你層狀分析結構，讓你順利跟著語音指令操作按鍵，一步步獲得需要的服務與協助。

最上層主選單通常先選擇語言種類：

❶ For service in (language), press (number).
（語言）服務，請按（數字）。

例 For service in English, press 1.
英語服務，請按 1。

次層包含許多選項選擇需要的服務、轉接、重聽、回上層或結束：

❷ For (service), press (number).
需要（服務），請按（數字）。

例 For sales, press 8.
需要業務服務，請按 8。

❸ To speak to (who), please press (number).
與（誰）通話，請按（數字）。

例 To speak to a customer service representative, please press 9.
與客服代表通話，請按 9。

❹ To hear these options again, please press (number).
重聽選項，請按（數字）。

例 To hear these options again, please press 2.
重聽選項，請按 2。

press [prɛs] *v.* 按；壓
representative [rɛprɪ`zɛntətɪv] *n.* 代表

❺ To return to the previous menu, press (number).
重回上層選單，請按（數字）。

例 To return to the previous menu, press 5.
重回上層選單，請按 5 。

❻ To end this call, please press (number).
結束通話，請按（數字）。

例 To end this call, please press 0.
結束通話，請按 0 。

如果你沒有做任何選擇，系統可能會出現下列這兩句：

❼ If you know the extension number of the person you are trying to reach, enter it now or stay on the line to speak to ...
如果您知道您要找的人的分機號碼，請現在輸入，或留在線上與……通話。

例 If you know the extension number of the person you are trying to reach, enter it now or stay on the line to speak to a customer service representative.
如果您知道您要找的人的分機號碼，請現在輸入，或留在線上與客服代表通話。

❽ To speak directly with a (person), please remain on the line.
要直接與（某人）通話，請留在線上。

例 To speak directly with a sales representative, please remain on the line.
要直接與業務代表通話，請留在線上。

menu [ˋmɛnju] *n.*（項目）主選單；菜單
enter [ˋɛntɚ] *v.* 鍵入；輸入

次層做好選擇後，系統常會要求輸入資料以便辨識：

❾ If you are (type) customer, press (number).

如果您是（種類）型客戶，請按（數字）。

例 If you are a <u>corporate</u> customer, press 123.

如果您是企業型客戶，請按 123 。

❿ Enter your (number) on the <u>keypad</u>, followed by the <u>pound key</u>.

請在鍵盤上輸入您的（號碼），接著請按 # 字鍵。

例 Enter your customer number on the keypad, followed by the pound key.

請在鍵盤上輸入您的顧客編號，接著請按 # 字鍵。

系統辨識完身份後，下一層可能要求你再做選擇：

⓫ If you know the extension of the person you are trying to reach, press (number).

如果您知道您要找的人的分機號碼，請按（號碼）。

例 If you know the extension of the person you are trying to reach, press 1.

如果您知道您要找的人的分機號碼，請按 1 。

⓬ For (service), (service) or (service), press (number).

需要（服務）、（服務）或（服務），請按（數字）。

例 For sales, customer support or to check the status of your order, press 588.

需要業務服務、客服或查詢您的訂單狀況，請按 588 。

corporate [ˋkɔrpərɪt] *adj.* 公司的；團體的

keypad [ˋki͵pæd] *n.* 小型鍵盤（如電話或計算機的）

pound key [ˋpaʊnd ͵ki] *n.* 井字鍵 (#)

科技日新月異，人類社會的發展總是朝著更完善的方向邁進，電話語音系統也是。語音辨識系統「聽」命行事，免除鍵盤操作，造福行動不便的人與盲胞。

⑬ For service in (language), please say (language).
需要（語言）服務，請說（語言）。

例 For service in English, please say "English."
需要英語服務，請說「英語」。

系統可能列出幾項需求提供選擇：

⑭ Please choose one of the following three options: ...
請從以下三個選項當中選擇一個：……。

例 Please choose one of the following three options: sales, customer support, or shipping.
請從以下三個選項當中選擇一個：業務、客服或出貨。

這項科技需要努力突破的地方在於「辨識精確度」；由於每個人的說話方式及語調都不一樣，每個地區的發音、用詞及腔調亦不盡相同，因此容易造成電腦辨識的困難。

⑮ Did you say (system guess)? If yes, please say "yes." If not, please say "no."
您說的是（系統猜測）嗎？是的話，請說「是」；不是的話，請說「不是」。

例 Did you say, "sales"? If yes, please say "yes."
您說的是「業務」嗎？是的話，請說「是」；不是的話，請說「不是」。

⑯ I didn't understand what you said. Did you say (system guess)?
我無法辨識您說的話。您是不是說（系統猜測）？

例 I didn't understand what you said. Did you say, "sales?"
我無法辨識您說的話。您是不是說「業務」？

儘管這項科技仍未臻完善，相信專家會繼續努力研發、力求進步。

2 實戰時間 Show Time

2.1

我們在前面的必通句型單元已經層狀分析過語音指令，接下來的兩篇語音系統回覆裡各有個小小的測驗要測試一下你的熟練度。

Thank you for calling Sundance Systems.

For service in English, please press 1. For service in German, please press 2. For service in Spanish, please press 3. For service in Chinese, please press 4. For service in Japanese, please press 5.

If you are a corporate customer, press 1. If you are an individual customer, press 2. If you are a joint customer, press 3. If you are a supplier, press 4. If you are a manufacturer, press 5.

If you know the extension of the person you are trying to reach, press 1. For sales, customer support or to check the status of your order, press 2. To speak to a customer service representative, please press 3. If you require immediate assistance, please press 4. To return to the main menu, please press 5. To hear these options again, please press 6. To return to the previous menu, press 7. To end this call, press 0.

To speak with a shipping representative, press 1. To speak to a sales representative, press 2. To speak to customer support, press 3.

If you have an order number, please enter it now on the keypad, followed by the pound key. If you have not received an order number, please press 1. If the order is incorrect, please press 2. To discuss your order with a shipping representative, please press 3.

Hi, this is Robert ... your shipping representative. How can I help you today?

Yes, this is Eric Jackson of All-U-Want Megastore in the States. I need to know the shipping date of our orders.

請問 Eric Jackson 按了哪些號碼才轉到 Robert ？

2.2

Thank you for calling Morton Electronics.

If you know the extension number of the person you are trying to reach, enter it now or stay on the line.

Please choose one of the following three options: sales, customer support, or shipping. I didn't understand what you said. Did you say, "sales?" If yes, please say "yes." If not, please say "no."

Are you a new customer, an existing customer, or a corporate customer?

Please say your corporate account number now.

I didn't understand what you said. Could you please repeat your corporate account number?

Did you say "5-8-0-0-2-1-6?" If yes, please say "yes." If not, please say "no."

Thank you.

Is your company located in Asia, Europe, or North America?

Please stay on the line and a North American corporate account sales representative will be with you as soon as possible.

Your business is important to us. Please stay on the line and a customer service representative will be with you shortly.

Please remain on the line. We are currently experiencing a large volume of calls. Your call will be answered faster if you remain on the line than if you call back.

Hello. This is Richard. How may I be of assistance?

請依序選出來電者說過的字：

sales, customer service, shipment, shipping, customer support

no, yep, not, none, yes

new customer, regular customer, existing customer, business partner, corporate customer

5800214, 5810316, 5700216, 5800216, 5800612

North American, Asia, Europe, South America, North America, America

譯文 2.1

日舞系統感謝您的來電。

英語服務，請按 1 ；德語服務，請按 2 ；西班牙語服務，請按 3 ；中文服務，請按 4 ；日語服務，請按 5 。

如果您是企業型客戶，按 1 ；如果您是個人客戶，按 2 ；如果您是聯名客戶，按 3 ；如果您是供應商，按 4 ；如果您是製造商，按 5 。

如果您知道您要找的人的分機號碼，請按 1 ；需要業務服務、客服、或查詢您的訂單狀況，請按 2 ；與客服代表通話，請按 3 ；如果您需要立即協助，請按 4 ；重回主選單，請按 5 ；重聽選項，請按 6 ；重回上層選單，請按 7 ；結束通話，請按 0 。

與出貨代表通話，按 1 ；與業務代表通話，按 2 ；與客服通話，按 3 。

如果您有訂單編號的話，請現在輸入鍵盤，接著請按 # 字鍵；如果您還沒有收到訂單編號的話，請按 1 ；如果訂單有誤，請按 2；要與出貨代表討論您的訂單，請按 3。

您好，我是羅勃特……，您的出貨代表。 我今天能提供您什麼協助？

是的，我是美國應有盡有量販店的艾瑞克・傑克森。我需要知道我們訂單的出貨日期。

Word List

individual [ˌɪndə`vɪʤʊəl] *adj./n.* 個人（的）
joint [ʤɔɪnt] *adj.* 聯合的；共有的
megastore [`mɛgəstor] *n.* 一種貨品種類繁多，購物方式類似超級市場的大賣場
the States [ðə `stets] *n.*（非正式）美國 (= the USA)

Answer: 1, 1, 2, 1, 3

譯文 2.2

謝謝您打電話來摩頓電子。

如果您知道您要找的人的分機號碼，請現在輸入，或留在線上。

請從以下三個選項當中選擇一個：業務、客服或出貨。

我無法辨識您說的話。您是不是說「業務」？是的話，請說「是」；不是的話，請說「不是」。

您是新客戶、現有客戶，還是企業型客戶？

請現在說出您的企業客戶編號。

我無法辨識您說的話。您能不能重複一次您的企業客戶編號？

您是說「5-8-0-0-2-1-6」嗎？是的話，請說「是」；不是的話，請說「不是」。

謝謝。

貴公司在亞洲、歐洲或是北美洲？

請留在線上，北美洲的企業客戶業務代表將盡快為您服務。

您的事情對我們非常重要，請留在線上，客服代表很快就會為您服務。

請留在線上。我們目前承接大量來電，如果您留在線上的話，您的電話將比您再打一次更快得到回應。

您好，我是理察。我能提供什麼協助？

Word List

existing [ɪg`zɪstɪŋ] *adj.* 現存的；現行的
be located in ... 位於……
large volume of sth. 大量的某事物（volume [`vɑljəm] *n.* 量）

Answer: sales, yes, corporate customer, 5800216, yes, North America

小心陷阱

☹ 錯誤用法

Please **stay online** and a **sale** representative will **come** as soon as possible.

請留在線上，業務代表將盡快為您服務。

☺ 正確用法

Please **stay on the line** and a **sales** representative will **be with you** as soon as possible.

請留在線上，業務代表將盡快為您服務。

文化小叮嚀

When doing business in New Zealand, always be on time—punctuality is extremely important. Additionally, business discussions are typically not appropriate during dinner, which is a social occasion with little conversation. However, business discussions are fine during lunch.

在紐西蘭做生意時，永遠要準時——守時格外地重要。此外，晚餐期間通常不適合討論業務，因為這是個鮮少進行對話的社交場合。然而，午餐的話就可以放心討論業務。

Word List

New Zealand [ˌnju ˋzilənd] *n.* 紐西蘭

punctuality [ˌpʌŋktʃuˋælətɪ] *n.* 守時

appropriate [əˋproprɪˌet] *adj.* 適當的

3 實戰演練 Practice Exercises

I 請為下列兩題選出正確的中文譯義。

❶ pound key

(A) 保留鍵 (B) 米字鍵 ＊ (C) 井字鍵 ＃

❷ main menu

(A) 主菜單 (B) 主選單 (C) 單據

II 請根據你聽到的內容為下列三題選出正確解答。

❶ What extension number should the caller enter if he or she wants to place an order?

(A) 11

(B) 13

(C) 14

❷ Which number should the caller enter if he or she is a regular contributor to Alpha and has something to discuss with his or her responsible editor?

(A) 10

(B) 11

(C) 13

❸ Which number did the caller press?

(A) 15

(B) 12

(C) none

＊解答請見 244 頁

總複習
Final Call

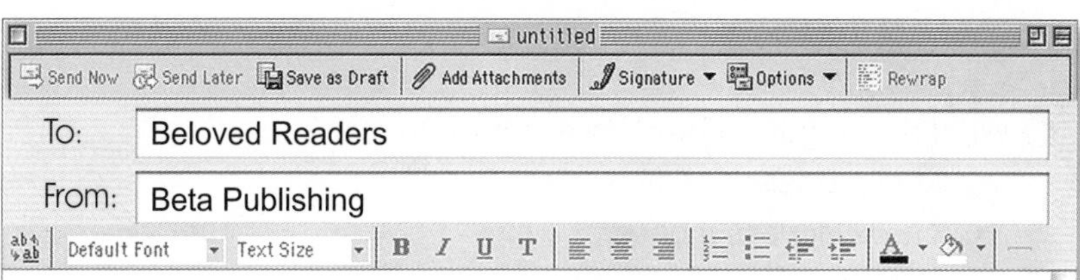

Dear readers:

This chapter is a review of all 15 previous chapters. We hope you have enjoyed your reading, listening, and learning so far. Let's see how much progress you've made from the book. Please listen to the following conversation (CD II-26) and finish the exercise that follows this page.

Thank you for your support and we hope you can continue with us.
Beta Multimedia Publishing

親愛的讀者：

本章是前面 15 章的總複習，我們希望到目前為止您的閱讀、聽力與學習都很愉快。我們來看看您藉由這本書進步了多少。請聽接下來的對話（CD II-26），完成這一頁之後的練習。

謝謝您的支持，希望您能夠繼續指教。
貝塔語言出版

Grand Finale 精采完結

CD II-26

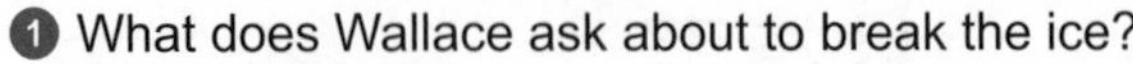

1. What does Wallace ask about to break the ice?
   (A) The economy.
   (B) The weather.
   (C) How Roland is doing.
   (D) All of the above.

2. What new product does Wallace have to offer?
   (A) A new, smaller memory stick.
   (B) A new wireless mouse.
   (C) A new wireless keyboard.

3. What doesn't Roland like about the keyboard that Wallace sent him?
   (A) The reception is poor.
   (B) The feet slip.
   (C) The keys stick.

4. What is Roland's number one concern?
   (A) Logo placement.
   (B) Feet that don't slip.
   (C) Price.

5. When does Roland want to discuss the new memory sticks?
   (A) After he's fixed the logo problem.
   (B) After they agree on a price.
   (C) After he sees the product sample.

6. Why does the telephone conversation end suddenly?
   (A) Because they have covered everything.
   (B) Because Roland has a meeting.
   (C) Because Wallace has another call.

＊對話內容請見 246 頁
＊解答請見 254 頁

實戰演練
Answer Keys

Chapter 1 取得聯絡

I 1. (C) 2. (B) 3. (B)

II 1. (A) 2. (B)

CD I-05

A: Scott Enterprises. May I ask who is calling?

B: Hello, this is David Walker of Next Electronics.

A: How can I help you, Mr. Walker?

B: Could I have Donald Jacobsen, extension 898, please?

A: Certainly. Wait just a moment while I transfer you.

A: 史考特企業，請問您哪位？

B: 您好，我是耐斯特電子的大衛・沃克。

A: 沃克先生，我能幫你什麼忙嗎？

B: 能不能幫我接唐納・嘉可森，分機 898 ，麻煩你？

A: 當然。稍待片刻我幫您轉。

❶ 誰打電話給史考特企業？

(A) 大衛・沃克。

(B) 史考特・嘉可森。

(C) 大衛・安德森。

❷ 接著會發生什麼事？

(A) 沃克先生會打電話給史考特企業。

(B) 沃克先生會和嘉可森先生講話。

(C) 嘉可森先生會打電話給耐斯特電子。

III 範例解答：

Hi, this is Priscilla McKim of Frontier Electronics in Taiwan. I would like to speak with the sales manager, Don Williams.

Mr. Williams, I am calling in regard to a short meeting you had with our VP, Mr. Toffler, at the Berlin Consumer Electronics Trade Fair. Mr. Toffler told me that you expressed interest in purchasing our CD burners and flash drives.

您好，我是台灣開拓電子的普莉西亞・麥金。我想和業務經理唐・威廉斯講話。

威廉斯先生，我打電話過來聯絡關於您和我們副總裁陶福勒先生在柏林消費性電子展的簡短會談。陶福勒先生告訴我，您對購買我們的光碟燒錄機和隨身碟表示興趣。

burner [ˋbɝnɚ] *n.* 燒錄機

flash drive [ˋflæʃ ˏdraɪv] *n.* 隨身碟（或稱 thumb drive [ˋθʌm ˏdraɪv]）

接聽來電

I 1. (B) 2. (C) 3. (C)

II 1. (C) 2. (B)

Good morning. Speedy Systems. How can I help you? Exports Department? Who are your looking for? May I ask your name? Wallace Kuo of Omega Electronics in Taiwan? Thanks, Mr. Kuo. May I ask the purpose of your call? Well, Mr. Kuo, I believe you should talk to our Imports Department. Please hold while I direct you to Ms. Gray in Imports.

早安。速必遞系統。我能幫您什麼忙嗎？出口部門？您要找誰？可以請問您是哪位嗎？台灣歐美嘉電子的瓦勒斯．郭？謝謝，郭先生。能否請問您這通電話的目的是？嗯，郭先生，我想您應該跟我們的進口部門聯絡才對。請稍等，我幫您轉給進口部的葛瑞小姐。

1 來電者來自哪間公司？

(A) 速必遞系統。

(B) 出口部門。

(C) 歐美嘉電子。

2 這通電話會被轉到哪裡？

(A) 給歐美嘉電子的葛瑞小姐。

(B) 給進口部門的葛瑞小姐。

(C) 給出口部門的葛瑞小姐。

III 範例解答：

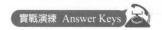

I'm sorry, Ms. McKim. Mr. Wang is out of the office and I'm not sure when he'll be back. Can I take a message, or would you like Mr. Wang to call you back?

對不起，麥金小姐。王先生現在不在辦公室，我也不確定他什麼時候會回來。您要不要留話我代為轉告，還是您希望王先生回電給您？

Word List

export [`ɛksport] *n.* 出口；輸出
import [`ɪmport] *n.* 進口；輸入

Chapter 3 建立關係：閒聊

I 1. (C) 2. (C) 3. (C)

II 1. (A) 2. (B)

CD I-13

Paul: Hi Daniel. How is the economy in Taiwan these days?

Daniel: Thanks for asking, Paul. Better than last year, but still not that strong. I think our GDP will grow by about 3% this year.

Paul: How are things there? You just had a 3-day weekend, didn't you?

Daniel: Yes. Didn't I tell you what I did last weekend?

Paul: No. What did you do?

Daniel: I took the whole family to the mountains for a skiing trip. It was fantastic.

保羅： 嗨，丹尼爾。近來台灣的經濟怎麼樣？

丹尼爾：謝謝你問起，保羅。比去年好，但是仍然不是那麼強勁。我想今年我們的國內生產總值會成長約百分之三。

保羅： 那你那裡的情況如何？你剛放完三天的周末假期，不是嗎？

丹尼爾：是啊。我沒有跟你說我上週末做了什麼嗎？

保羅： 沒有。你做了什麼？

丹尼爾：我帶全家人上山做了趟滑雪之旅。真是棒呆了。

❶ 台灣的經濟怎麼樣？

(A) 比去年好。

(B) 沒去年好。

(C) 跟去年一樣。

❷ 丹尼爾上週末做了什麼？

(A) 他去山裡健行。

(B) 他跟他的家人去滑雪。

(C) 他三天週末假期去台灣玩。

III 範例解答：

Do you know what I did last weekend? I went to Hong Kong to the Asian Computer Show. It was really great. Have you ever been to Hong Kong?

你知道我上週末做了什麼嗎？我去香港參觀亞洲電腦展。真的很棒。你有沒有去過香港？

GDP 國內生產毛額；國內生產總值（gross domestic product [`gros də`mɛstɪk `prɑdəkt] 的縮寫，爲一國或一地區境內在一定的期間內所生產的物品與勞務總值，是反映經濟生產活動成果的一個綜合性指標）

fantastic [fæn`tæstɪk] *adj.*（口）很棒的；非常好的

Chapter 4 轉入正題

I 1. (C) 2. (C) 3. (B)

II 1. (C) 2. (B)

CD I-17

Terry: Jonathan, I've got a meeting I have to attend. Is there anything in particular you want to discuss?

Jonathan: Yes, Terry. Let me give you my list of issues I think we need to discuss.

Terry: Sure, let me get a pen.

Jonathan: I'd like to reach a decision on order quantities, shipping options, and delivery dates by the end of this week.

Terry: Shouldn't be a problem. I'll send you my proposal for each issue by email, and then we can talk Thursday afternoon to confirm your order.

Terry: OK, sounds good. Talk to you then.

泰瑞： 強納森，我有一個會議要參加。你有任何特別的事想討論的嗎？

強納森：有，泰瑞。讓我告訴你我認為我們需要討論的幾個議題。

泰瑞： 好，讓我拿支筆。

強納森：我希望這個週末前能就訂單數量、送貨方式的選擇及交貨日期做出決定。

泰瑞： 應該不是問題。我會用電子郵件把我對每項議題的提案寄給你，然後我們可以在星期四下午確認你的訂單。

強納森：好，聽起來不錯。到時候再聊。

❶ 強納森想在這個週末前決定好什麼？

(A) 貨物的價格。

(B) 貨物的型號。

(C) 貨物的交貨日期。

❷ 泰瑞什麼時候會寄電子郵件給強納森？

(A) 星期四下午。

(B) 星期四下午以前。

(C) 他們講完電話後的幾分鐘之内。

III 範例解答：

There are a couple things we need to talk about. Do you mind if we discuss the size of the order first. Then we can talk about the product specs, timeline and shipping details.

有幾件事情我們需要討論。你介不介意我們先討論訂單的數量？然後我們可以談產品規格、時間表和出貨細節。

Word List

decide on (sth.) 考慮後決定（爲某事物）

model [`mɑdḷ] *n.* 型號；樣式；模型；模範

quantity [`kwɑntətɪ] *n.* 數量；量

proposal [prə`pozḷ] *n.* 提議；計劃；提案

Chapter 5 聚集焦點

I 1. (B) 2. (B) 3. (C)　　II 1. (C) 2. (B) 3. (C)

CD I-21

Greta: Sylvia, I still have a couple of questions regarding payment terms. Can we revisit the payment terms again?

Sylvia: I thought we settled on those during our last discussion. But sure, tell me what's wrong with them.

Greta: Well, in our last discussion, we agreed to pay cash in advance.

Sylvia: Yes, as our Purchasing Department informed you earlier, we need an advance cash payment to buy raw materials since they will need to be custom-made for this order. Normally we use materials from another supplier that we have been working with for a long time.

Greta: Oh ... According to the decision made this morning by our financial manager I'm afraid that we will have to change the payment terms to CAD.

Sylvia: That may cause us some problems. I need to talk with our purchasing manager and get back to you.

Greta: When can I expect your call?

Sylvia: No later than tomorrow noon.

Greta: OK.

葛瑞塔：絲薇亞，關於付款條件我還是有一些問題。我們能不能再回到付款條件？

絲薇亞：我以為我們已經在上次的討論當中決定好那些事情了。不過當然，告訴我它們有什麼問題吧。

葛瑞塔：嗯，在我們上次的討論中，我們同意以預付現金的方式付款。

絲薇亞：是的，如同我們採購部門稍早通知妳的，我們需要一筆預付現款來購買原物料，因為它們是為了這張訂單而特別訂製的。通常我們都使用另一個我們已經合作很長一段時間的供應商的原物料。

葛瑞塔：噢……根據我們財務經理今早所做的決定，恐怕我們必須將付款條件改成付現交單。

絲薇亞：那可能會對我們造成一些問題。我需要和我們的採購經理談一下再回電給妳。

葛瑞塔：我什麼時候能期待妳的回電？

絲薇亞：最晚不超過明天中午。

葛瑞塔：好。

❶原本同意的付款方式是什麼？

(A) CAD。

(B) <u>COD</u>。

(C) Cash in Advance。

❷誰做了決定更改付款條件？

(A) 生產經理。

(B) 財務經理。

(C) 採購經理。

❸絲薇亞可能會在什麼時候回電給葛瑞塔？

(A) 明天晚上。

(B) 明天下午。

(C) 明天早上。

III 範例解答：

All these issues are <u>interrelated</u>. I think we should return to our discussion about product colors before we discuss logo <u>placement</u>, as the colors will impact both the logo size and placement. We have access to the complete rainbow of colors, but I think we can eliminate the softer colors <u>right off the bat</u> — they just don't match our <u>corporate image</u>.

這些議題全都有相互關係。我想在討論商標擺放位置之前，我們應該回到我們對產品顏色的討論，因為顏色對商標尺寸和擺放位置都會產生影響。我們有完整七彩可以選擇，但我想我們可以立即淘汰較柔和的顏色——它們實在不符合我們的企業形象。

Word List

settle on (sth.) 選定（某事物）
cash in advance 【商】預付現金
raw materials [ˋrɔ məˋtɪrɪəlz] *n.*（常用複數）原物料
custom-made [ˋkʌstəmˏmed] *adj.* 訂製的
supplier [səˋplaɪɚ] *n.* 供應商
CAD 【商】付現交單；憑單據付款（Cash Against Documents 的縮寫）
COD 【商】貨到付款（Cash On Delivery 或 Collect On Delivery 的縮寫）
interrelated [ˏɪntɚrɪˋletɪd] *adj.* 有互相關係的
placement [ˋplesmənt] *n.* 定位；配置
right off the bat 立即；一開始
corporate image [ˋkɔrpərɪt ˋɪmɪdʒ] *n.* 企業形象

Chapter 6 總結重點

I 1. (B) 2. (B) 3. (C)

II 1. (A) 2. (A)

CD I-25

Paula: What are you trying to say?

Dwight: I'm saying that we are going to have to change the product.

Paula: Well, I think that maybe we should consider changing the product specs, but I don't think we should touch the design.

Dwight: There's a lot more that needs to be changed than just the specs, believe me.

寶拉： 你想說的是什麼？

杜威特：我說的是我們將必須修改產品。

寶拉： 嗯，我想也許我們應該考慮改變產品規格，但我不覺得我們應該去碰設計。

杜威特：需要改變的比光是規格多多了，相信我。

❶ 這位男士想做什麼？

(A) 對產品做大規模修改。

(B) 對產品規格做小幅度修正。

(C) 用不同的方式行銷產品。

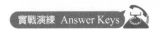

❷ 這位女士認為產品的什麼需要被修改？

(A) 其規格。

(B) 其設計。

(C) 其價格。

III 範例解答：

What I am saying is that we need some assurance that the product will be here on time. If it's late, we will lose money and our <u>competitors</u> will get our customers. So, I guess we need to know some more about your production schedule, and even more importantly, we need some assurance that we will get the shipment on time.

我說的是我們需要一些保證確定產品會準時送到這裡。如果遲了，我們就會損失金錢，而我們的競爭對手則會得到我們的顧客。所以，我想我們需要再多瞭解一下你們的生產進度，更重要的是，我們需要一些保證確定我們將準時收到貨。

Word List

competitor [kəm`pɛtətɚ] *n.* 競爭者；對手

Chapter 7 結束通話

I 1. (C) 2. (B) 3. (A)

II 1. (B) 2. (C)

CD I-29

Marcus: I hope I've been of some assistance.
Hana: Believe me, you have been, but I still have some questions.
Marcus: OK, but I'm sorry. I've got to run in about 10 minutes. Do you think we can cover your questions in that time, or should we make another appointment?
Hana: I think we have time now.

馬克斯：我希望我所做的有所幫助。
漢娜：相信我，有，但我還是有一些問題。
馬克斯：好，但對不起，我大概過 10 分鐘後必須離開。妳覺得我們能在這段時間內解決妳的問題嗎，還是我們應該另外約一個時間？
漢娜：我想我們現在有時間。

❶ 這位女士要什麼？
(A) 感謝男的幫忙。
(B) 再問幾個問題。
(C) 在幾分鐘之內離開。

❷ 接著會發生什麼事？

(A) 女的會和男的約定另一個約會。

(B) 男的會離開。

(C) 女的會再問男的幾個問題。

III 範例解答：

John: Hi, Jerry, this is John. I haven't heard from you since we talked last week and I just wanted to touch base with you about the contract negotiations.

Jerry: I'm glad you called, John. I was just going to give you a ring myself. I just sent the revised contract to you this morning.

John: You did? Fantastic. That's what I needed to know.

Jerry: Is that all, then? I need to get going if I'm going to make my next meeting.

John: I think that covers it. Talk to you soon.

強： 喂，傑瑞，我是強。自從我們上個禮拜說完話後我就沒有你的消息，我只是想跟你聯絡有關合約的談判。

傑瑞：很高興你打電話過來，強。我正想自己打通電話給你呢。我今早剛把修改過的合約寄過去給你。

強： 真的？太棒了。我就是需要知道這個。

傑瑞：那，沒其他的事了吧？我得走了，如果我想趕上下一個會議的話。

強： 我想差不多就這樣了。下次再聊。

revised [rɪˋvaɪzd] *adj.* 校正過的；修訂過的

與你的客戶或同事共事

I 1. (B) 2. (C) 3. (B) 4. (B)

II 1. (B) 2. (A)

CD I-33

Paul: What are the chances that you could send the memory stick color changes to the manufacturer today?

Sue: Today? I don't think that will be a problem.

Paul: I also want to take a minute and revisit the product specifications.

Sue: Sure, let's do that. Where should we start?

保羅：你能在今天把記憶卡顏色的更改送去給製造商的可能性有多大？

蘇： 今天？我想那不會是個問題。

保羅：我還想用一點時間重新檢視產品規格。

蘇： 沒問題，再看一遍吧。我們該從哪裡開始？

❶ **這位男士要這位女士做什麼？**

(A) 改變記憶卡的顏色。

(B) 聯絡製造商。

(C) 改變產品規格。

❷ 這位男士和這位女士接下來會談什麼？

(A) 產品規格。

(B) 顏色的更改。

(C) 記憶卡的問題。

III 範例解答：

Before we end this meeting, let's go through the action items one more time. First, we need a signed contract ASAP, hopefully before this coming Monday. Second, the shipping deadline is the 14th. No delays are allowed unless someone can pay the penalty for us. And third, the handling charge will be reduced by 5%.

在我們結束這個會議之前，讓我們再看一遍行動項目。第一，我們需要一份簽署好的合約，愈快愈好，希望能在接下來的這個星期一之前。第二，送貨期限是十四號，不容許延誤，除非有人能替我們付罰金。第三，手續費會減少 5 % 。

Chapter 9 釐清問題

I 1. (A) 2. (C) 3. (C) 4. (B)

II 1. (A) 2. (B)

CD II-04

Katrina: There aren't any changes to product colors that I need to know about, are there?

Paul: No, we are staying with those colors. But we changed our minds about the order size.

Katrina: No problem. What are the changes?

Paul: We've decided to <u>double</u> the quantity of the 512GB <u>chips</u> and <u>halve</u> the quantity of the 256 GB chips.

Katrina: So, that's 20,000 of the larger ones, and 5,000 of the smaller ones?

Paul: That's right.

卡翠娜：沒有任何有關產品顏色的改變是我需要知道的吧，有嗎？

保羅：沒有，我們就用那些顏色。但是我們改變了我們對訂單數量所做的決定。

卡翠娜：沒問題。有哪些改變？

保羅：我們決定要把 512 GB 晶片的數量增加一倍，把 256 GB 晶片的數量減半。

卡翠娜：所以，就是 20,000 片較大的晶片，和 5,000 片較小的晶片？

保羅：沒錯。

❶ 保羅想改變訂單的哪一方面？

(A) 晶片的數量。

(B) 產品的顏色。

(C) 晶片的大小。

❷ 保羅想訂購多少片 512 GB 的晶片？

(A) 10,000 。

(B) 20,000 。

(C) 5,000 。

III 範例解答：

As a result of the increased cost of oil, we might need to revisit our pricing policy in order to minimize the effect on our profits. If some of our customers change their minds and decide to reduce their orders, there's no penalty if they modify them before February 12th.

由於原油的成本上漲，為了盡量減少對利潤所造成的影響，我們可能需要重新討論我們的定價政策。如果有客戶改變他們的決定並選擇減少訂單，只要他們在二月十二日之前修改就不須支付違約金。

Word List

double [ˋdʌbḷ] *v.* 增加一倍

chip [ʧɪp] *n.* 晶片；積體電路片

halve [hæv] *v.* 將……減半；將……拆半

penalty [ˋpɛnḷtɪ] *n.* 罰款；處罰

Chapter 10 闡明議題

I 1. (A) 2. (C) 3. (C)

II 1. (C) 2. (B)

CD II-08

Pam: So there won't be any changes to the order, correct?

Davis: Well, cost and delivery date will both change.

Pam: OK. You've lost me. Can you explain what you meant before about no changes?

Davis: Well, there will be changes to cost and the delivery date, but not to the style or quantity of products being ordered.

潘：所以訂單不會有任何改變，對嗎？

戴維斯：呃，成本和交貨日期都會變。

潘：好。你把我搞糊塗了。你能解釋一下你先前說的沒有改變是什麼意思嗎？

戴維斯：嗯，成本和交貨日期會變，但訂購的產品款式或數量不會。

❶訂單的什麼部份將改變？

(A) 產品款式。

(B) 產品數量。

(C) 交貨日期。

❷這位男士先前說「沒有改變」時，他是什麼意思？

(A) 他的意思是訂單絕對不會有改變。

(B) 他的意思是訂單的某些部分不會變。

(C) 他的意思是成本會變，但交貨日期不變。

III 範例解答：

Let me repeat this back to you to make sure there are no mistakes. The quantity of this order is 2,000 pieces, shipping date September 15th, FCA to San Francisco. But I'm a bit confused about the payment details, and so I'm hoping you can clarify. As I recall from our last discussion, you will wire half of the payment as deposit and clear the balance in three months. Is that right?

讓我向您重複一遍以確定沒有任何錯誤。這份訂單的數量是 2,000 件，出貨日期九月十五日， FCA 到舊金山。但我對付款細節有點困惑，所以我希望您能說明一下。我記得根據我們上次的討論，你們會匯一半的款項當作訂金並於三個月結清餘款。這樣對嗎？

FCA【商】貨交送貨人條件 + 指定地名（Free Carrier (... named place)，指賣方必須在規定的期限內，將貨物送到指定交貨地點買方所指定的運送人收；若買方未明確指定交貨地點，賣方可在規定的地方或區域內，選定運送人接管貨物的地點爲交貨地點；此交易條件於貨櫃、海、空、鐵公路運輸皆適用）

wire [waɪr] *v.* 匯款

deposit [dɪ`pɑzɪt] *n.* 訂金；押金；存款

balance [`bæləns] *n.* 餘額；平衡；協調

Chapter 11 解決問題

I 1. (B) 2. (C) 3. (B)

II 1. (A) 2. (C)

CD II-12

Max: Kim, what if we decided to cut shipping costs by 10%? Would that work?

Kim: I think that would work, Max, as long as the shipment arrives on the same date.

Max: This is a complicated situation. What is the most important factor for you? Is it the shipping cost or the shipment arrival date?

Kim: Both are important, but the shipment absolutely needs to be delivered by the date we originally discussed.

麥克斯：金，如果我們決定減少 10% 的運費呢？這樣可行嗎？

金：我想可以，麥克斯，只要貨物在同一個日期抵達就行。

麥克斯：這是個複雜的情況。對你們來說最重要的因素是什麼？是運費還是貨物的抵達日期？

金：兩個都重要，但貨物絕對必須在原先我們討論的日期前抵達。

❶ 麥克斯願意提供什麼？

(A) 減少運費。

(B) 提早交貨日期。

(C) 產品價格的折扣。

❷ 金要求什麼？

(A) 運費減少 20% 。

(B) 較早的交貨日期。

(C) 運費減少 10% 和原先的交貨日期。

III 範例解答：

Mr. Lin, I have discussed the situation with my manager to see if there are any alternatives to the current proposal. What if we accommodate your most recent request and reduce the shipping costs by 25%? I've looked at all the options, and that is the best we can do. Will that work for you?

林先生，我已經和我的經理談過這個情況，看是不是有任何選擇可以取代目前的提案。如果我們因應你們的最新要求並將運費減少 25% 呢？我已經考慮過所有的選擇，這是我們能做的極限了。對你們而言可行嗎？

Word List

proposal [prə`pozḷ] *n.* 提議；提案；求婚

Chapter 12 計劃電訪

I　1. (C)　2. (B)

II　1. (C)　2. (B)

CD II-14

Ryan:　Rhoda, is delivery next week possible?

Rhoda:　Sure. This week would be a little rushed, but next week should be no problem. Monday is a holiday, but you should have it on Tuesday.

Ryan:　Can you send me the <u>tracking number</u> for the shipment?

Rhoda:　I'll fax the shipment <u>confirmation</u> to you on Thursday morning after the shipment goes out.

萊恩：蘿妲，下個禮拜交貨可能嗎？

蘿妲：當然。這個禮拜有點太趕，但下個禮拜應該沒有問題。禮拜一是假日，但是你們禮拜二應該拿得到。

萊恩：妳能把貨運的追蹤號碼寄給我嗎？

蘿妲：貨出了之後我會在星期四早上把出貨確認書傳真給你。

❶ 為什麼無法在星期一交貨？

(A) 有點太趕。

(B) 郵局星期一不營業。

(C) 星期一是假日。

❷ 蘿妲什麼時候會把追蹤號碼傳送給這位男士？

(A) 星期一早上。

(B) 等貨被送出後。

(C) 星期二。

III 範例解答：

I want to talk to you about the next generation of two of our products: the bluetooth mouse and keyboard. Sales of regular keyboards and mice have been dropping dramatically, and almost everyone is moving away from them. All of our clients have had great success with our wireless versions, though. Do you have time to hear about them?

我想跟你聊一下我們兩樣產品的新版本：藍芽滑鼠與鍵盤。一般鍵盤與滑鼠的銷量已經劇幅下跌，幾乎每個人都快不使用它們了；然而，我們的無線版本讓我們的客戶全都獲得重大的成功。你有時間瞭解一下它們嗎？

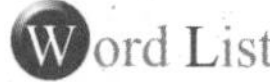

tracking number [`trækɪŋ `nʌmbɚ] *n.* 追蹤號碼（貨物寄出後核發的號碼，以備有問題時可追查）

confirmation [ˏkɑnfɚ`meʃən] *n.* 確認

bluetooth [`bluˏtuθ] *n.* 藍芽（一種通訊無線傳輸技術）

Chapter 13 留言

I 1. (C) 2. (A) 3. (B)

II 1. (A) 2. (C)

CD II-18

Daniel: Hello, this is Daniel Baker, general manager of Jasper Construction. I'm out of the office right now, but if you leave your name and number I'll get back to you as soon as I can.

Pamela: This is Pamela Duff from Actus Enterprises, and I'm calling to leave a message for Mr. Daniel Baker of Jasper Construction. Mr. Baker, I'd like you to know that we're prepared to accept your terms, as long as we can negotiate a 30-day extension on our payment due date. That means you would receive payment 60 days after the shipment arrives at our warehouse. Please call me back on my mobile phone at 0953-543-793. Thanks.

丹尼爾：您好，我是傑室博建設的總經理丹尼爾・貝克。我現在不在辦公室，但如果您留下您的姓名與電話，我會盡快回電給您。

潘蜜拉：我是艾克特斯企業的潘蜜拉・道芙，我打電話來留言給傑室博建設的丹尼爾・貝克先生。貝克先生，我想讓您知道我們已經準備好接受您的條件了，只要我們能夠商定付款期限延緩三十天。那就是您將在貨物抵達我們倉庫後的六十天收到款項。請打我的手機 0953-543-793 回電給我。謝謝。

❶ 潘蜜拉跟丹尼爾是什麼關係？

(A) 她是個潛在的客戶。

(B) 她是個潛在的供應商。

(C) 她是個潛在的雇主。

❷ 潘蜜拉想在什麼時候支付貨款？

(A) 當它們被送達時。

(B) 它們被送達後 30 天。

(C) 它們被送達後 60 天。

III 範例解答：

It's Clay Potter calling from National Instruments on Tuesday, April 17. I need to discuss the new order with you. I still have a few questions that I need answers to. I'm hoping we can talk no later than next Monday. It would be great if you can get back to me earlier. My number is 1-212-632-8049. Thanks.

我是克雷．波特，四月十七號星期二從國際儀器打電話過來。我需要和你討論新訂單的事，我還有一些問題需要解答。我希望我們最晚不超過下星期一談，如果你能更早回電給我的話更好。我的號碼是 1-212-632-8049 。謝謝。

general manager [ˌdʒɛnərəl ˋmænɪdʒɚ] *n.* 總經理

construction [kənˋstrʌkʃən] *n.* 建造；建築物

instrument [ˋɪnstrəmənt] *n.* 儀器；樂器；工具

打電話開發

I 1. (B) 2. (C) 3. (C)

II 1. (B) 2. (A)

CD II-22

Sheila: I'm sorry. Who is this again?

Paul: I just told you. This is Paul Myers of Activa Electronics.

Sheila: Oh, right, Mr. Myers. I meant to ask you the last time. Do you sell memory sticks?

Paul: No, we don't sell memory sticks.

Sheila: Just what do you sell, then?

Paul: We mostly focus on keyboards and LCD monitors.

席菈：對不起。請再說一次你是誰？

保羅：我剛才才說過。我是艾克提瓦電子的保羅・邁爾斯。

席菈：喔，對，邁爾斯先生。我上次就想問你。你們有沒有賣記憶卡？

保羅：沒有，我們不賣記憶卡。

席菈：那你們賣的是什麼？

保羅：我們主要銷售鍵盤和液晶螢幕。

❶ 為什麼這位女士要問這位男士是誰？

(A) 他們之前從來沒說過話。

(B) 她不記得他是誰。

(C) 她忘記他在哪裡工作。

❷ 這位男士的公司賣什麼？

(A) 液晶螢幕。

(B) 記憶卡。

(C) 滑鼠。

III 範例解答：

My name is Jane Robertson. I'm with Robust Appliance, a leader in electrical housewares and kitchen supplies. I'm sure you get a lot of cold calls, but if you can lend me a few minutes, I believe I can show you how to dramatically increase your company's sales revenue this year. I have a batch of new, brand-name mixers which I'm prepared to unload at the lowest price on the market. Would you like to hear some more details?

我的名字叫珍・羅柏森。我在羅霸司特家電工作，我們是家電用品及廚房用具的領導品牌。我相信您一定常接到許多推銷電話，但如果您能借我幾分鐘的時間，我相信我一定能告訴您如何劇幅地增加貴公司今年的業績收入。我手上有一批新的名牌攪拌機，我準備用市面上最低價脫手。您想聽取更多細節嗎？

Word List

robust [rə`bʌst] *adj.*（物）堅固耐用的

appliance [ə`plaɪəns] *n.* 器具；設備

electrical [ɪ`lɛktrɪkḷ] *adj.* 用電的；電動的

housewares [`haʊsˏwɛrz] *n.*（複數形）家庭（尤指餐廚）用具

supplies [sə`plaɪz] *n.*（複數形）供應品；生活用品

dramatically [drə`mætɪkḷɪ] *adv.* 戲劇性地

revenue [`rɛvəˏnju] *n.* 收益；稅收

a batch of things/people 一批東西／人

brand-name [`brændˏnem] *adj.* 名牌的

mixer [`mɪksɚ] *n.* 攪拌機；攪拌器

unload [ʌn`lod] *v.*【商】抛售；脫手

操作電話語音系統

I 1. (C) 2. (B)

II 1. (C) 2. (B) 3. (C)

Thank you for calling Alpha Publishing. If you know the extension number of the person you are trying to reach, enter it now. For the editorial department, press 11. For the marketing department, press 12. For the planning department, press 13. For sales, press 14. For customer service, press 15. For the operator, please stay on the line. ... Please hold while we connect you to the operator.

第一出版感謝您的來電。如果您知道您要找的人的號碼，請現在輸入。轉接編輯部，請按 11 ；行銷部，請按 12 ；企劃部，請按 13 ；業務部，請按 14 ；客服，請按 15 。如要與總機通話，請留在線上。……請稍候，我們將為您轉接總機。

❶ 如果來電者想下訂單的話，他或她應該按什麼分機號碼？

(A) 11

(B) 13

(C) 14

❷ 如果來電者是第一定期的投稿者，有問題想和他或她的責任編輯討論的話，應該按哪個號碼？

(A) 10

(B) 11

(C) 13

❸ 來電者按了哪個號碼？

(A) 15

(B) 12

(C) 沒按

contributor [kən`trɪbjutɚ] *n.* 投稿人；捐獻者

Chapter 16 總複習

CD II-26

Wallace dials Roland's number.

Automated Answer: Thank you for calling Ubertech. For service in German, please press 1. For service in English, please press 2. For service in French, please press 3. For service in Japanese, please press 4. ...

If you know the extension of the person you are trying to reach, enter it now. For sales, press 1. For production, press 2. For shipping, press 3. To speak to a customer service representative, press 4. ... (Chap. 15)

Wallace dials Roland's extension.

Roland: Roland Kuhn speaking.

Wallace: Roland, it's Wallace. How are you doing?

Roland: Great. How are you?

Wallace: Pretty good. How's the weather in Berlin? (Chap. 3)

Roland: Rainy. It's a very wet winter. How are things in Taiwan?

Wallace: About the same, cold and wet. Listen, I wanted to touch base with you on how our products are moving. (Chap. 4) But I guess I should first ask you about how the economy in Germany is these days? (Chap.3)

Roland: It's a bit slow. Things have been better.

瓦勒斯撥打洛藍的號碼。

自動答覆：優博科技感謝您的來電。德語服務，請按 1 ；英語服務，請按 2 ；法語服務，請按 3 ；日語服務，請按 4 。……

如果您知道您要找的人的分機號碼，請現在輸入。業務部，按 1 ；生產部，按 2 ；出貨部，按 3 ；與客服代表通話，按 4 。……（第 15 章）

瓦勒斯按了洛藍的分機號碼。

洛藍： 我是洛藍・昆。

瓦勒斯：洛藍，我是瓦勒斯。你好嗎？

洛藍： 很好。你好嗎？

瓦勒斯：很好。柏林天氣好嗎？（第 3 章）

洛藍： 常下雨。今年冬天很多雨。台灣一切好嗎？

瓦勒斯：也差不多，一樣寒冷、潮濕。聽著，我想跟你聯絡討論關於我們產品的動向。（第 4 章）但我想我應該先問你德國最近的經濟怎麼樣？（第 3 章）

洛藍： 有點冷清，以前比較好。

Wallace: Sorry to hear that. Things are a little slow here as well. But I'm sure they'll pick up pretty soon. Roland, I know it's late in the day in Berlin, so let me get right down to business. (Chap. 4)

Roland: Sure. You wanted to talk about sales?

Wallace: It sounds like I already have my answer. I also wanted to talk to you about our next generation of memory sticks.

Roland: To be honest, we are not moving a lot of memory sticks.

Wallace: Well, this new model is the smallest 1-gigabyte stick on the market.

Roland: I think that size will have a considerable effect on consumer interest. (Chap. 5)

Wallace: That's what we were thinking when we designed it.

Roland: Wallace, is it possible that you could send me a sample that I can show our marketing team? (Chap. 8)

Wallace: Sure. Did you get a chance to show them the wireless mouse and keyboard?

Roland: Yes, I did. They have a number of concerns. First, they are concerned with the size of the mouse. Second, they have an issue with the angle of the keyboard.

瓦勒斯：聽到你這麼說很難過。我們這裡的情況也有點蕭條，但我想很快就會改善。洛藍，我知道現在在柏林時間很晚了，所以我就立刻切入正題吧。（第 4 章）

洛藍： 好。你想談銷量？

瓦勒斯：聽起來我好像已經有答案了。我還想跟你聊一下我們新一代的記憶卡。

洛藍： 老實說，我們的記憶卡銷售動得不多。

瓦勒斯：呃，這個新型號是市面上最小的 1GB 記憶卡。

洛藍： 我想尺寸大小對消費者是否會有興趣的影響會很大。（第 5 章）

瓦勒斯：我們在設計的時候就是這麼想的。

洛藍： 瓦勒斯，你有沒有可能可以寄一個樣品給我，我可以拿給我的行銷團隊看？（第 8 章）

瓦勒斯：當然可以。你有機會把無線滑鼠與鍵盤拿給他們看了嗎？

洛藍： 有，我給他們看過了。他們有一些考量。首先，他們很在意滑鼠的大小。第二，他們對鍵盤的角度有意見。

Wallace: Roland, I don't understand what you mean by the angle of the keyboard. (Chap. 10)

Roland: Well, the keyboard rests flat on a table top. If you want it to sit at an angle, then you pop out the small feet at the top. But these feet are plastic, so they tend to slide across the table.

Wallace: OK. I understand. You are not happy with the feet on the keyboard.

Roland: That's correct. The only concern with the mouse is that it is too small. What we are looking for is a medium-size mouse. (Chap. 6)

Wallace: Let's go through this list of concerns again. (Chap.8) You are not happy with the feet on the keyboard and the size of the mouse. You are looking for a medium-size mouse.

Roland: That's right. And we think that the price you quoted for the keyboard is a little high. And we'd like it if we had a few options for logo placement.

Wallace: If we provide more options for logo placement, it's going to affect the price. (Chap. 9) What is the most important issue for you? (Chap. 11)

Roland: Of course, price is the No. 1 issue. (Chap. 6) But we also need options on logo placement and better feet.

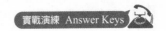

瓦勒斯：洛藍，我不懂你說的鍵盤的角度是什麼意思？（第 10 章）

洛藍：　呃，鍵盤原本是平整地放在桌面上的。如果你想用角度把它立起來，就必須把頂端的小腳架扳出來。但這些腳架是塑膠做的，所以很容易在桌上打滑。

瓦勒斯：好，我懂了。你們不滿意鍵盤的腳架。

洛藍：　沒錯。對滑鼠的唯一考量就是它太小了。我們在找的是尺寸適中的滑鼠。（第 6 章）

瓦勒斯：我們再把這張考量清單看過一遍。（第 8 章）你們對鍵盤的腳架和滑鼠的大小不滿意；你們在找中尺寸的滑鼠。

洛藍：　沒錯。而且我們認為你那個鍵盤報的價格有點高。還有，我們比較希望商標的擺放位置能有一些選擇。

瓦勒斯：如果商標擺放的位置我們提供更多選擇的話，會影響到價格。（第 9 章）對你們而言最重要的議題是什麼？（第 11 章）

洛藍：　當然，價格是首要議題。（第 6 章）但我們也需要商標擺放位置的選擇和更好的腳架。

Wallace: A lot of your product concerns are interdependent. Let's deal with logo placement first. (Chap. 4) Where exactly do you want the logo?

Roland: Well, we'd like to have an option of top right, top left, and on the shift key.

Wallace: I'll see if I can minimize the effects these changes will have on final price. (Chap. 9)

Roland: I'd appreciate that.

Wallace: Are there any issues you want to discuss regarding the memory sticks? (Chap. 7)

Roland: Can we discuss this later, after I've had a chance to look at the sample? (Chap. 7)

Wallace: Sure, no problem.

Roland: Listen, Wallace, I have meeting in 5 minutes I have to attend. (Chap. 7)

Wallace: OK. That just about covers it. Call me if you have any problems. (Chap. 7)

Roland: OK. Take care. Talk to you soon.

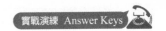

瓦勒斯：你們對產品的考量有許多是息息相關的。讓我們先處理商標放的位置。（第 4 章）商標你們確切想擺在什麼地方？

洛藍：　呃，我們希望能選擇放在右上方、左上方或字型變換鍵上。

瓦勒斯：我看我是不是能把這些改變對最後價格的影響減到最低。（第 9 章）

洛藍：　我很感謝你這麼做。

瓦勒斯：關於記憶卡你還有任何其他問題想討論的嗎？（第 7 章）

洛藍：　我們能不能晚點再討論這個，在我有機會看過樣品之後？（第 7 章）

瓦勒斯：當然，沒問題。

洛藍：　聽著，瓦勒斯，我 5 分鐘後有個會議必須參加。（第 7 章）

瓦勒斯：好。差不多都說到了，如果你有任何問題就打電話給我。（第 7 章）

洛藍：　好，保重。我很快就會跟你談。

(trade or the economy) pick up（商業或經濟）改善；進步
sb. is concerned with sth. 某人擔心、掛慮某事
rest [rɛst] *v.* 支撐在……；擱在……
pop out *phr. v.*（使）彈出
plastic [`plæstɪk] *adj.* 塑膠（製）的
slide [slaɪd] *v.* 滑動；滑行
shift key [`ʃɪft ˏki] *n.*（電腦或打字機鍵盤上的）字型轉換鍵

Grand Finale: 1. (D) 2. (A) 3. (B) 4. (C) 5. (C) 6. (B)

1. 瓦勒斯問洛藍什麼來開場？
   (A) 經濟。
   (B) 天氣。
   (C) 洛藍的近況。
   (D) 以上皆是。
2. 瓦勒斯必須提供什麼新產品？
   (A) 一款新的、更小的記憶卡。
   (B) 一款新的無線滑鼠。
   (C) 一款新的無線鍵盤。
3. 洛藍不喜歡瓦勒斯寄給他的鍵盤的什麼地方？
   (A) 收訊很差。
   (B) 腳架會滑。
   (C) 鍵盤會卡鍵。
4. 洛藍的首要考量是什麼？
   (A) 商標擺放位置。
   (B) 不會滑的腳架。
   (C) 價錢。
5. 洛藍什麼時候才想討論新記憶卡？
   (A) 等他解決商標問題之後。
   (B) 等他們同意價格之後。
   (C) 等他看過產品的樣品之後。
6. 為什麼電話談話突然中止？
   (A) 因為他們該說的都已經涵蓋到了。
   (B) 因為洛藍有個會議。
   (C) 因為瓦勒斯有插播。

break the ice 打開話題；打破沉默（如在派對或會議上）

slip [slɪp] *v.* 滑動；滑掉

key [ki] *n.*（鋼琴、打字機等的）鍵；鑰匙

fix [fɪks] *v.* 解決（問題）；決定（價格、日期等）；修理；安排

BIZ English 系列

第一套為台灣上班族量身定做的商用英文指南

搞定英文面試

1書1CD 定價：220元

- 30 句面試最實用對話
- 50 個面試最常見問題
- 80 個表現個人特質的最佳字彙
- 110 個面試重點歸納

搞定產品簡報

1書2CD 定價：350元

- 40 個描述產品的好用詞彙
- 40 幅肢體語言的範例圖示
- 80 個講解圖表數據的相關句型
- 120 個運用視覺教具的必備用語

搞定商務口說

1書2CD 定價：350元

- 40 個最常見談判範例
- 80 個介紹公司最常用字彙
- 80 個必通簡報句型
- 120 個必通電話用語

搞定談判英文

1書2CD 定價：350元

- 72 個常見周旋情境
- 200 個談判關鍵用語
- 795 句談判必通句型
- 以「情境學習法」模擬談判過程

搞定口說錯誤

1書2CD 定價：320元

- 150 則生活會話錯誤
- 150 個易混淆字詞
- 300 則職場用語不當
- 450 則最易犯口說錯誤全羅列

搞定接待英文

1書2CD 定價：320元

- 16 個接待最常見情境
- 31 個擬真對話範例
- 388 個拉近距離好用句
- 250 個招待在地遊加分字彙

＊相關系列「 BIZ English for Busy People 」已陸續出版，敬請期待！

喚醒你的英文語感！

國家圖書館出版品預行編目資料

搞定商務電話= Biz Telephoning / Bill Hodgson作；諸葛蓓芸 譯.——初版.——臺北市：貝塔, 2006〔民95〕 面； 公分

ISBN 957-729-564-9（平裝附影音光碟）

1. 商業英語—會話

805.188 94025161

搞定商務電話

Biz Telephoning

作　　者 / Bill Hodgson
總 編 審 / 王復國
譯　　者 / 諸葛蓓芸
執行編輯 / 邱慧菁

出　　版 / 貝塔語言出版有限公司
地　　址 / 100 台北市館前路12號11樓
電　　話 / (02)2314-2525
傳　　真 / (02)2312-3535
郵　　撥 / 19493777貝塔出版有限公司
客服專線 / (02)2314-3535
客服信箱 / btservice@betamedia.com.tw

總 經 銷 / 時報文化出版企業股份有限公司
地　　址 / 桃園縣龜山鄉萬壽路二段 351 號
電　　話 / (02) 2306-6842

出版日期 / 2006年1月初版一刷
定　　價 / 320元
ISBN：957-729-564-9

貝塔網址：www.betamedia.com.tw

喚醒你的英文語感！

後釘好，直接寄回即可！

廣　告　回　信
北區郵政管理局登記證
北台字第14256號
免　貼　郵　票

100 台北市中正區館前路12號11樓

貝塔語言出版 收

Beta Multimedia Publishing

寄件者住址 □□□

謝謝您購買本書！！

貝塔語言擁有最優良之英文學習書籍，為提供您最佳的英語學習資訊，您可填妥此表後寄回（免貼郵票）將可不定期收到本公司最新發行書訊及活動訊息！

姓名：__________________ 性別：□男 □女 生日：____年____月____日

電話：(公)________________(宅)________________(手機)________________

電子信箱：____________________________________

學歷：□高中職含以下 □專科 □大學 □研究所含以上

職業：□金融 □服務 □傳播 □製造 □資訊 □軍公教 □出版
□自由 □教育 □學生 □其他

職級：□企業負責人 □高階主管 □中階主管 □職員 □專業人士

1. 您購買的書籍是？________________________

2. 您從何處得知本產品？(可複選)

   □書店 □網路 □書展 □校園活動 □廣告信函 □他人推薦 □新聞報導 □其他

3. 您覺得本產品價格：

   □偏高 □合理 □偏低

4. 請問目前您每週花了多少時間學英語？

   □ 不到十分鐘 □ 十分鐘以上，但不到半小時 □ 半小時以上，但不到一小時
   □ 一小時以上，但不到兩小時 □ 兩個小時以上 □ 不一定

5. 通常在選擇語言學習書時，哪些因素是您會考慮的？

   □ 封面 □ 內容、實用性 □ 品牌 □ 媒體、朋友推薦 □ 價格□ 其他________

6. 市面上您最需要的語言書種類為？

   □ 聽力 □ 閱讀 □ 文法 □ 口說 □ 寫作 □ 其他__________

7. 通常您會透過何種方式選購語言學習書籍？

   □ 書店門市 □ 網路書店 □ 郵購 □ 直接找出版社 □ 學校或公司團購
   □ 其他__________

8. 給我們的建議：____________________________________

____

喚醒你的英文語感！

Get a Feel for English !

喚醒你的英文語感！

Get a Feel for English !